SWEPT

AWAY

A Regency Fairy Tale

Vanessa Riley

Books by Vanessa Riley

Madeline's Protector

Swept Away, A Regency Fairy Tale

Sign up at VanessaRiley.com for contests, early releases, and more.

Copyright © 2014 Vanessa Riley

Published by BM Books
A Division of Gallium Books
Suite 236B, Atlanta, GA 30308

ISBN: 9907437-1-2

ISBN-13: 978-0-9907437-1-2

Charlotte Downing, the Duchess of Charming, wants what she wants. Today, it's a fine pair of lacy slippers crafted by the renowned Ella's Establishment. To be picture perfect for her presentation to the queen, Charlotte will survive crashed ceilings and falling bricks. Yet, has she met her match in the conservative merchant, whose autumn-colored eyes make her pulse race, especially when he says *no*?

Caught between the glittering world of the *ton* and the respectable profession of selling shoes, Edwin Cinder can't understand the lady's persistence or the fire lighting her blue eyes when she's challenged. With his lack of pedigree, there's no chance for this common God-fearing man to win her hand, but he'll risk all to save the duchess from the ravages of a London gale.

Swept Away is a Regency retelling of Cinderella with a twist.

Dedication

I dedicate this book to my Copy Editor Supreme, my mother Louise, my loving hubby Frank, and my daughter Ellen. Their patience and support have meant the world to me.

I also dedicate this labor of love to critique partners extraordinaire: June, Mildred, Lori, Connie, Gail.

My mentor, Laurie Alice, for answering all my endless questions.

And my team of encouragers: Sandra, Michela, Piper, and Panya.

Cast of Primary Characters

Charlotte Downing, the Duchess of Charming, is the daughter of the late Duke of Charming.

Mr. Edwin Cinder, who is called Cinder or Mr. Cinder, is the owner of the Ella shoe stores. The stores are named after his late mother, Ella Cinder.

Mercy Goodmom is Charlotte's companion. A companion is not a servant, but she goes with the duchess as a chaperone and friend.

Ella Cinder, Edwin's mother, was the driving force for the Ella shoe stores, running the stores until Edwin came of age. She married Lord Rundle, which gave her the title Lady Rundle or the Countess Rundle.

Lady Lillian Theol is the daughter of Lord Rundle and Ella Cinder (Countess Rundle).

Shelby Theol is the Baron Rundle, also called Lord Theol. He is Lord Rundle's heir. Being his heir, Shelby Theol will eventually inherit the earl's title and possessions.

Lord Rundle is the Earl of Rundle. He is Baron Rundle and Lady Lillian Theol's father. He's Edwin's stepfather.

Abraham is Lord Rundle's butler. He manages Fairwilde, Lord Rundle's home. Lady Lillian and Lord Theol also live at Fairwilde.

William St. Landon is the Duke of Cheshire. He is also known as Lord Cheshire or Cheshire. He is a friend of Charlotte's father, the Duke of Charming, as well as Lord Rundle.

CHAPTER ONE

London, March 3, 1818

Only one thing frustrated Charlotte Downing more than waiting on a man: being told "no" by one. With the shoe clerk from Ella's Establishment refusing her purchase without the owner's permission, she'd suffered both. Tapping her foot, she stifled the urge to shift upon her chair. The shopkeeper could return any moment, and she shouldn't appear too anxious. That would expose weakness, maybe doubling the price. If her late father taught her anything, it was never cede anything early in a negotiation.

Her gaze lifted to the pair of fairy slippers displayed on an upper shelf of the Ella Store. Protected by a clear glass case, the footwear remained isolated, distant. A little like herself, especially during her lengthy time of mourning.

She blinked, then imagined fingering the

crystals-tasseled to the sides and the velvet bows lining the gilded heel. Her heart raced. Those shoes had to become hers. If she'd ever known love, surely it would feel like this, palms perspiring with expectation.

She'd watched enough of Father's dealings to know how to get her way. The shop owner wouldn't stand a chance against a Downing. Right?

Doubt swirled inside her chest. Could she be as good as the late duke at anything? She pressed at her bodice, smoothed her tightening collar, and returned her thoughts to her goal. Charlotte, the new Duchess of Charming, would sweep low and curtsy for the queen in those shoes. Everyone would study her court dress of white silk, with its trims of scarlet and pearls. They'd eye her traipsing in those beautiful slippers and accept Charlotte as a picture of grace and elegance.

The gossip would certainly arrest.

Look at the girl with the man's title.

How much did the old duke pay the Mad King to keep his legacy?

Moisture dampened her lashes. She batted her lids and fanned her brow, anything to stave off a full cry. Everything still hurt—losing Father, being left to figure things out alone. What to do of his charities? They'd traveled so much, where should she make her home?

Mercy Goodmom, her companion, moved from the rattling store window. With a push at the wide cinnamon-colored banding of her bonnet, she tipped it backward and tugged an escaping brunette curl. "The wind outside nearly blew me away. Must we....Oh my." Mercy rushed to her side and pulled out a handkerchief. "Duchess, don't go getting worked up. Think of the yummy hot chocolate we sipped at the coffeehouse."

Charlotte took the soft lawn cloth and dabbed at her face. "We had a good day roaming the streets of Cheapside, outrunning our cluster of attendants."

She patted her mouth, her kid gloves smearing moisture about her face. Not very regal. Definitely nothing a duchess should do.

Her companion shook her head, dug into her over-sized reticule, and yanked out another handkerchief. She dusted the pristine chair next to Charlotte's and plopped on its seat. "We've stayed too long. Time to go back where we belong."

Mercy's way of almost singing a rebuke was both endearing and loathsome.

Where exactly did Charlotte belong? The town house filled with all her father's expedition treasures? The country home layered with his papers and books? Everywhere, bits of him remained, reminding her of how much he fashioned every aspect of her life.

Stomach churning, she siphoned a slow breath. "If I am to be presented at court..." Charlotte's voice sounded low, wispy to her ear. She cleared her throat, raised her tone. "It must be on my terms."

"Oh, I hate that look in your eyes, the wild stare. Nothing but trouble comes next. The slippers aren't worth it." Her companion fished in her bag again and pulled out a paper-wrapped bonbon, popping the sugary treat into her mouth.

"Is it five yet, Mrs. Goodmom? The owner should be back by now."

Crunching and munching, Mercy nodded.

Where was he? Setting her umbrella on the spotless pine floor, Charlotte popped up. The hem of her dark gray skirts swished about her short boots as she rushed toward the shelving displaying her slippers.

"Look at these, Mercy. The stitching, the crystals. Is there a better pair? I think not." They were fine enough for dancing, to skip and twirl about a properly chalked floor. At a distance, one might even think the white gems matched the beading on her gown.

She fingered the glass.

Mercy's rotund silhouette appeared at her side. "You put too much energy on this and overtask yourself. Next thing you know, you'll be sick and can't attend your presentation."

She'd not miss this one. With both parents dead, and no close relations, there wouldn't be a reason to delay this meeting. "Don't even think such heresy. I will be presented this time."

Her companion folded her arms and gazed toward the window. "We should go out tonight for fun. We need a practice before the big day. I know, the Fairwilde soiree, the Rundle invitation."

Father's friend? More stories of how great Father was. As if she didn't know of his acclaim. "I will go out for Friday's presentation. It's the day I return to society with these slippers."

Mercy put a hand to her hip. With her chestnut-brown spencer, she looked like one of the mugs from the coffeehouse they'd just left. "Duchess, I wish you would get flustered over attending an entertaining dinner, or dare I say a man—not shoes."

Charlotte swiped at her brow then glanced at her heart's desire trapped in glass. "Well, if I could wear a gentleman on my feet and be as stylish, he might do."

The door to the shop blew open, letting in a harsh blast of wind before slamming shut. Her heart raced as icy air swept through her, chilling down to her chemise. The weather wouldn't hold up much longer. Where was the person in charge?

With a huff, Mercy offered a toothy smile, one inflated by candy bliss. Well, dear Mercy was sweet enough without the added sugar. "You don't have to outdo him you know. Even the duke could accept 'no.'"

A knot lodged in Charlotte's throat. There was so much to prove to the world. And from heaven, the always-right, always-in-control man had to be watching, judging her. "Father was formidable. Only death stopped him from getting what he wanted. I'm not dead."

Mercy squinted. "Your time of mourning ended last week. You can dress as you like, do whatever it is you want. That includes not continuing to dress as a martyr."

Charlotte folded her arms and tugged on her sleeves. The dark wool of her half-mourning gown had become a protective layer, allowing her to beg off from outings and all the uncomfortable things in her life.

It let time stand still as she embodied a dutiful daughter honoring her father, not a girl lost. *Lord, what is it I am called to do?*

No answer. Just the screech of the wind slamming against the window.

Wasn't silence an answer?

Filling her lungs with the scent of tangy wood polish and resolve, she squared her shoulders. "I have a picture in my mind of my come-out, particularly the way I'll look. It will be so."

Pulling on the slackened ribbons of her bonnet, she marched to the attendant's stand and tapped on the maple top until the clerk returned from the back room. "Is the proprietor returning? We've waited quite a long time, almost an hour."

"Ma'am." The short fellow scratched his bare skull. "He should 'a been back by now." His gaze lifted. "The weather must be delaying him, but trust me. He'll not sell those slippers. I could make ye a similar pair, but it will take two weeks."

When he was alive, Father had always stared a man in his eyes. She leaned over to catch the clerk's gaze. "Two weeks is too long. I need them Friday."

"It's Tuesday. Shoes don't magically appear. No mice in the back workin' all night." The man chuckled, pushed his spectacles back upon his short nose. "Mice." He laughed again, then disappeared to the rear.

She let her hand go limp, dropping and then swatting the counter. How could the answer be no? "Why display shoes if they aren't to be sold?"

Fingers tapping, she pondered her arguments for the proprietor—that is, if he showed. The answer would be no for someone else, but not Charlotte. She was every bit as astute as her father, so she couldn't be dissuaded.

"We'll come back tomorrow." Mercy raised her palm to her eyes and looked outside. "So dark and gray. The overcast skies will catch us if we stay any longer. Well, maybe it won't last long, or we could nap here."

"Tomorrow. I'll possess these shoes." She moved to the door, but half-pivoted toward the back of Ella's. Strengthening her voice, she made a final stand. "Good sir, let the owner know to expect us at the start of business."

As she rotated to exit, the door to the shop opened and a man bounded inside. He forced his collar down. "The weather's..." His autumn-brown eyes locked with hers. A dimple showed on his heart-shaped face. "The weather's very strange."

Her pulse stopped as a wide smile appeared upon his lean countenance.

"Ladies." The tall gentleman in onyx and snow-white evening wear dipped his top hat, an expensive, familiar thing. "Be careful. The clouds are ready to burst."

"Then we must go." Mercy took the lead and grabbed Charlotte's arm. She had to be quite concerned, for the woman didn't flirt with the handsome man, not once.

"Ladies." With one hand, he opened and held the door. With the other, he balanced his chapeau. Given the cut of its short cylinder and

the tidy inch of banding about its circumfer-
ence, it had to be constructed by Papa's favorite
haberdasher.

The lump returned and all she could do
was blink away the stirred sense of loss.

Mercy towed her forward. "Tomorrow, we
agreed. No second thoughts."

The wind ramped, clanging the overhead
signs strewn along Fish Street Hill. Charlotte
wrapped her arms tighter about her middle and
trudged toward their carriage parked along
Gracechurch. The walk seemed extra cold, as
she held no paper bundle of her treasured shoes
within her mitts.

The howl of the growing gale warbled the
panes of glass forming Ella's street front. Edwin
leaned against the door, hoping to catch a final
glimpse of the ladies. It wasn't dark yet, but the
two shouldn't be walking alone in this weather.

Perhaps he should run and catch up to
them and escort them to their transport. That's
what a gentleman would do, but Edwin wasn't
gently born.

How did his elder stepbrother put it? *A
product of low birth.*

It didn't matter that the trade of selling
shoes had restored Lord Rundle's circumstance
and continued to afford things such as twenty
shillings for a hat. Twenty.

He popped off the expensive thing and dusted the rich fabric upon his sleeve. A hat, more than a man's weekly wages?

For the sake of his stepfather, he'd bear the slights, buy costly headgear and linens, all to prove himself worthy of the man's respect.

With a final glimpse, he caught the blur of the young woman's dark skirt turning the corner. What if that was his dear sister, Lillian? Insides twisting, he tucked on his beaver dome and moved to straightening the shoe displays.

It wasn't Edwin's place to chase after a customer. Or to contemplate the tears gathering in her crystal blue eyes.

Not his place to be concerned for a class in which he didn't belong.

Straddling the gentry's, the merchants', and the workers' stations in society bore too much weight. Designing and selling shoes were comfortable to him, all he really knew. Happiness had to be in that.

"Mr. Cinder." Farmington, his clerk, stood at the counter with a bolt of tan kid leather. "The duchess and her companion will be here in the morn to convince you to sell the slippers. I tried to tell them we could make something similar, but you know how the genteel get."

"Perhaps she'll be in a better mood once the storm has passed. Bluster and foul moods go hand in hand." Edwin moved to his mother's wedding slippers, a pair he'd crafted with his own fingers and lasting tools. She prized the shoes, loved them with all her heart. Upon her deathbed, she wished them displayed here, in the store that made their fortune and her marriage to Lord Rundle possible.

Farmington rushed over with a duster and a stool. He wiped the glass container free of smudges. "Hopefully, they'll order a similar pair and be happy to wait for an Ella creation."

Farmington's words settled into Edwin's head. *Duchess, aye?* That might make the young lady a companion or better, a governess. A jolt went through him. Could those bluest of all eyes be in reach? "You say they'll return tomorrow?"

"Yes, sir." Farmington shoved his hands into the pockets of his dark apron. "Now go on. I can lock up. I see you are dressed for your stepfather's dinner." Stomach bulging, he stepped down and moved to the seating area. "Oh, one of the ladies left an 'mbrella. I'll hold it for them."

"No. They'll need it now. I'll see if I can return it. Goodnight." He scooped up the peach-colored thing by the pearl handle and rushed out the door. Nothing but catching the young lady and capturing her name filled his brain.

The wind chilled to the bone as he turned

the corner. Trotting, he scanned to the left and then the right. Which way had those pretty eyes gone?

His brand new top hat lifted from his brow, hurtling down the sidewalk. Grousing, he gave chase. Maybe it would lead him to the ladies. One could hope.

Wedged between a door and its frame, Edwin settled his long fingers upon the brim, but another arctic wind swept the commerce-filled street, sending the hat flying.

Lord, let it not splatter with mud. His stepfather would never forgive it. Lord Rundle was fastidious and noticed every mark or bit of lint.

Abandoning the sleek hat and arriving at his stepfather's party disheveled and ill-dressed would not bode well. The poor man would think Edwin didn't care for him or his opinions. That simply wasn't true.

Lord Rundle was a good man, a godly one, whose fussiness was only to make his children happy. And for some unknown reason, he treated Edwin well, even forcing him to go to tutors to speak like an equal to the man's gently bred sons.

Stomping, Edwin took the final steps. One swing of the umbrella knocked the hat from its nest in the chandler's sign. Twenty shillings. Oh, the lengths he endured to fit into Rundle's world, even for an evening.

Brim in hand, Edwin sped down an alley. The ladies had to be heading toward the mews. Another gust knocked him against the jeweler's window. If the weather grew any worse, the next wind would surely send him through, and he'd land flat on the gilded ostrich egg display. With his thick arms and torso, it would take all of Prinny's horses and men to put the fragile shells back together again.

Chuckling, he girded up his strength, pointed the umbrella like a walking stick, and trudged forward. As if moving on stilts, he balanced on his dancing leathers, his fine kid shoes stitched with brass buckles, and turned on to Gracechurch Street.

The ladies stood huddled together at the front of an alcove, no carriage in sight. They definitely needed assistance.

Above them, a draper's sign shook. The heavy wooden plank trembled with the ramping squall. The aged chains groaned, making the board shudder and knocking the brick facade.

"Ladies, I..." He'd only taken a step toward them when the creaking from above became deafening. *Snap. Wham.* His mouth dropped open.

The sign now dangled over their heads.

The tall one with the form of a lithe goddess froze, craning her long, thin neck to the overcast heavens. The danger must've hypnotized her, for she didn't move. Gold tendrils escaped her onyx bonnet.

Earlier, he'd been so captivated by her eyes, he hadn't noticed the color of her locks. Such a beauty, but an endangered one.

The short, buxom woman, the duchess, yanked on her young companion's dark sleeves to no avail.

"Take care!" His heart thudded in his chest as he sprinted. They could get hurt.

He saw no movement or acknowledgment of his warning. Perhaps the moans of the sign and the bellowing gale obscured it. The violent wind lifted the plank. The metal of the chains squealed. The links seemed to lengthen, then pull apart.

Arms outstretched, he rushed forward and grabbed each lady as if they were bolts of satin. Those lovely blue eyes, the bluest he'd ever seen, expanded as her fingers tangled along the silk of his waistcoat. With his awkward hold, he dragged them under the awning against the door.

Click. Pop. The ground shook as the massive sign hit the sidewalk. His tailcoat flapped against his legs from the rush of air. *Thank the Lord.* It missed them.

Something heavy, maybe a piece of the broken chain, slapped the back of his skull. Pain swept through him, darkening his vision. He sank against her bombazine skirt, sliding down to her trim ankles. He blacked out against the silk moiré ribbons of her slippers.

Charlotte shook free, letting her beleaguered rescuer flop from her feet to the ground. With a splat, the handsome fellow lay still, unconscious. She stooped and checked his head for injury, her fingers sweeping through his dark, curly mane. No cuts, just a lump the size of a melon.

"Will he live?" Mercy bent beside him, waving her meaty palm under his nose.

"I think so. But if he hadn't helped us…." A shudder raced Charlotte's spine. "I hate to think of the consequences." No more death.

Her friend knelt, whipped off the man's glove, then grabbed his wrist. Counting, she lifted it into the air.

So bold a move for a woman, touching a stranger. "What are you doing, Mercy?"

"I saw my father, Mr. Goodmom, do this to a patient."

Fidgeting, Charlotte folded her arms. She hated the helplessness settling in her cold fingers. The man could die while they fumbled. "Well?"

Mercy released him. "I'm not sure what it

means, but his hands are freezing."

"Mercy!" A sigh shot from Charlotte's mouth. Then she took a short breath, remembering Father's admonition: *dignity and calm are the start of all solutions*. In a firm but genteel tone, she said, "Let me revive him."

Kneeling, she swept off her own mitts and massaged his firm temples, then angled his strong jaw. This was the man they'd bumped into at Ella's—and he was holding her umbrella. Her heart sank. "He wouldn't be injured if I'd taken this with me."

She touched his neck. The vein pulsed with life. Who could he be? Did he know someone was looking after him?

Mercy leaned by Charlotte's ear. "Should we rifle through his pockets to see if we can find a name or a residence?"

Digging into his pockets didn't quite seem the lady-like, noble-woman thing to do. She shook her head. "I don't want him rousing, thinking he'd succumbed to footpads."

Was he breathing enough? Anguish clogged her throat, diminishing her voice to a whisper. "All this over shoes."

Mercy lifted her chin. "If it makes you feel better, they were some pretty shoes, fancy with beading."

Her fist balled and settled on the unconscious man's snowy cravat. "If the clerk at Ella's

Swept Away by Vanessa Riley

had just sold them to me when we first arrived, none of us would be here."

Her companion shrugged. "You have to respect a worker who follows orders."

Now that was ironic coming from Mercy. The woman didn't seem to know how to obey and still managed to catch each of Charlotte's inconsistencies. "We can't leave him here, Mercy."

Another strong wind whipped, off-balancing her. She slipped and struck the man's washbasin-hard stomach. "Sorry."

Mercy grabbed Charlotte's hands away, probably protecting the gentleman from further harm. "You get too worked up and fixed on things. Like staring at that sign or wanting those shoes."

The man released a deep moan. His eyes, an autumn-kissed brown with hints of gold, opened with heavy blinks.

She smoothed his upturned collar from his firm lips. "Where can we take you?"

He didn't answer. One of his hands lurched to his head. The movement was slow. His fingers vibrated in the harsh breeze.

"Let me help you as you helped us." Tentatively at first, then with nothing more than Papa's courage rattling her bones, she gripped his hand. "I will take you to a physician."

His bare palm tightened around hers.

"No…. to Rundle's…. Lord Rundle's." His hold became weak as his lids closed. The strong arm, which had sheltered her, fell away to the sidewalk.

Mercy stood and smoothed her spencer. "That's the dinner party you didn't want to attend."

"I didn't want to attend Fairwilde just because of my presentation." She wiped her mouth. "I might as well confess. Papa was attempting a match with one of the earl's son, but I'd heard those young men have grown up terribly wasteful." She pointed to her face. "With large noses."

His nose was well-proportioned, perfect for a man. She hadn't seen the sons, Shelby Theol and Percival Theol, in over fifteen years. Which one was this?

Her friend shook her head. "We shouldn't judge, for beauty's in the eye of the beholder." Mercy's lips lifted into a brilliant smile, the one she hid for schemes. "This one didn't inherit a large nose. Seems the late duke might have done well with a match to this heroic and handsome son."

Looking out at the vacant street, Charlotte pulled back, hoping to seem indifferent. She strengthened her voice. "Go get the footmen. He's not far from here. Then we'll take Mr. Theol to his father's."

Giggling, Mercy curtsied. "Yes, Duchess. And then we'll go freshen up and attend the party at Fairwilde, proper."

"Just go." Looks weren't everything. Her heart beat unevenly. The possibility that Papa could still orchestrate Charlotte's life from the grave was too much to bear, even if this man was noble and fiery handsome.

CHAPTER TWO

Fairwilde

The pounding in Edwin's head wouldn't quit. Nor would the feeling disappear that someone watched him. With a slow breath puffing out of his mouth, he opened one eye and then the other.

A smile grew on his young sister's oval face. Sweet, pale blue eyes fluttered beneath Lillian's full lashes. "You're awake. Brother, you scared us so."

Blinking, he swiveled his head. "Us?"

"Yes, sir." Abraham, Lord Rundle's butler, stood behind the sofa. The tall black man held a silver tray with wet towels.

A sweet scent reminiscent of dessert filled Edwin's nose. Was lemon ice wrapped in the cloth?

"Another cold one for the lump will do it,

Lady Lillian." Abraham lowered the tray for her.

Lillian reached and scooped the folded item. Cold water sprinkled from it onto Edwin's face. The liquid felt good.

"This might hurt." Her tiny finger squeezed underneath his aching skull, but soon the chilled rag eased the ache. The room slowed its rotation.

A thin blur came into focus. It bore his stepfather's shiny gold watch chain.

Edwin groaned at the pain coursing his body and at causing the man trouble the night of his big party.

"My goodness, boy." Lord Rundle swept at his perfectly coiffed gray locks and rose from a nearby chair. His wobbling legs seemed more unsteady. Had he been pacing, exerting himself before his soiree?

Rundle edged closer and lifted the cold rag from Edwin's temples. "Why, exactly, are you picking a fight with nature?"

Edwin tested his jaw, moving it up and down. "Obviously, I haven't the sense to know I'd lose."

Abraham shook his head. His dark mahogany eyes squinted, maybe too full of concern. The man hovered over the Theols as if they were his own family. Well, he'd been with them so long, maybe they were.

He tugged on his obsidian livery. "Sir, you shouldn't scare, Lord Rundle. The good man doesn't need such cares."

"Now, now. I'll interrogate him." His stepfather stepped near and patted Abraham's thick shoulder, then took a moment to straighten his man's collar. Rundle was such a stickler for proper etiquette. "Go check on the white soup. Fairwilde white soup is legendary."

"Yes, sir." The giant man nodded, tucked the shining platter under his arm, and plodded from the room.

Edwin wiggled his fingers, locking pinkies with Lillian, who still fussed about him.

She fluffed a cushion and patted his forehead. "No fever."

With a quick scan of his wrinkled waistcoat and rumpled pantaloons, his stomach flopped. The need for a basket grew urgent. Six quick breaths, followed by a long slow one, stopped his guts from forcing an exodus. "Lord Rundle, you must be horrified by my attire. Sorry, sir."

His stepfather came back into view. "When the footmen carried you in, I thought you'd been in your cups, but you don't drink like that. Not like your brothers."

"You mean stepbrothers." A harsh, gravel-filled voice sliced through the calm of the library. "Stepbrother." Lord Rundle's heir, the Baron Rundle named Shelby Theol, clomped inside. The loose floorboards creaked with each of his dragging steps until he rounded the sofa. "I heard the saint was in a scrap."

"I'm no saint, Theol. And 'twas no fight, unless you count a twenty-year-old falling sign darkening my daylights." Edwin touched the inch-wide lump on the back of his skull. "The board won."

"Brothers, stop. Edwin's a hero. He saved two ladies from certain death." Lillian grabbed her handkerchief and dabbed at her eye. Dramatic, romantic, pitchy thing. "And he could've been killed."

"No arguing." Lord Rundle flailed his hands then smoothed his tailcoat lapels. "I'm just... relieved Edwin's awake."

The poor man sounded winded. Hopefully the old fellow hadn't fretted too much.

"I'm going to check on the preparations." With almost a bounce in his gait, his stepfather's portly frame wobbled from the room. The burnished oak door closed with a gentle moan.

The warm room with its wall-to-wall bookshelves shuttered. A window popped open. Strong winds rattled everything. The odd storm must still be at play.

"My goodness." Lillian picked up her cream-colored skirts and pranced to the other side of the room, closing the pane. "Edwin, you mustn't pick fights with any more storms. It's like challenging God. Next time, you could be killed."

His stepbrother leaned over him, swinging a quizzing glass. One deep green eye narrowed behind the lens as the man's long hawk-like nose whipped up and down. His slicked raven curls, almost Lillian's hue, smoothed against his flat forehead as he leaned in for another inspection. "He appears very alive to me."

He poked Edwin's brow. "Well enough to leave and return back to the little shoe shop."

The pain blurring Edwin's vision made him imagine beating the stuffing out of the puffed-up gentleman. He closed his eyes. "Theol, I thank you for your concern, but I might accidentally latch my fingers about your neck to withstand the next wave of throbbing. Would that be fine?"

The quick thud of the Baron's low heels sounded of retreat. Good. At least the clown knew how far to push.

Thwack. The noise of a stiff cloth hitting something danced in Edwin's ear.

Peeking through his lashes, he watched their sister hit Theol again on the arm with her prized Oriental fan. Wonderful use of fabric.

"Both of you—especially you, Shelby Theol—need to quit squabbling." Her lips pursed together just like Mama's used to do.

"Yes, sister." His stepbrother rubbed his el-

29

bow, then leaned against the window. He might tolerate Edwin, but he did seem to care for Lillian. Half-blue blood must be good enough for the Baron.

The thin man stretched the curtains wide. The wind blew hard, making all the leaves of the nearby beech tree sail in a parallel line. Such strong gusts. This storm had already won against fist-sized chain links. What other damage would it do?

"The workmen aren't finished reappointing the brick. This storm will set their labors back. Well, I'm sure another bank note will ease the strain, right ... brother Cinder?"

Yes, Shelby would consider Edwin family when it came to the pocketbook.

"And they've yet to fortify the late countess's favorite room. The lady, your mother, loved it most of all. Pity if it languishes."

Theol wasn't dumb, just obnoxious. "Send the bills. I'll take a look."

The library was Mama's favorite room in Fairwilde. It felt cozy and warm in spite of the bluster created by the storm and his stepbrother. The good fire in the two-story mantel must be working hard to keep the winds at bay.

"Make an effort, Edwin." His sister's low whisper chilled his soul, an exact duplicate of Mama's tone and words.

With a grunt, he sat erect. When the world

stopped spinning, he lifted his chin toward his stepbrother. "Theol, I took your advice."

"What?" The man turned and sat against the sill. "You're selling the stores?"

The door to the library sprang open, and Lord Rundle plodded back inside. "Did I hear selling? Edwin, are you going to sell? I know the money did a great deal for us, but we're in a different position."

The grin on his stepfather's face stretched from ear to ear. "You should buy land and settle down."

Settle down? "I..." Truthfully, Edwin didn't know what he wanted. He was too educated and connected to mesh with the merchant class, but he didn't have the pedigree that the upper crust deemed a necessity to belong.

Head aching, he eased against the tufted sofa. The strong, sturdy comfort enveloped him. "Must we discuss this now? My skull's ablaze, and your party will begin in minutes."

Shelby snorted. "A brother in trade. Even a stepbrother is too much."

Edwin folded his arms, but snapped his lips shut. The anguish in Lillian's eyes stung. Why did she have to inherit Mama's love for family and the pale blue eyes, too?

Yet his gut knotted at the irony of his situation. Shoe-trade money staved off Rundle's bankruptcy. No one looked down upon Mama as she wrote the bank notes, which righted his accounts. And Theol would always soften as long as Edwin continued to draft them.

Swallowing gall, he gazed at the burgundy tapestry hanging above the mantel and shuffled his feet against the worn boards. He'd have to insist they repair the floors with the rest of the renovation. "The advice I followed was to visit your haberdasher. He fitted me quite fine."

Scanning to each side, Edwin didn't see the bothersome thing, made of top-notch beaver. "The hat must not have made the final trip."

"No." Lord Rundle retook his seat. "It did. The footmen are working to get the dust off it."

A smile arose on his stepfather's lean face. "It looked to be a beauty. Let's see how it fares once it's brushed out."

Theol nodded. "Nice to know you do listen. But Father, must we go through with this dinner party? The weather, which almost did the good shoemaker in, will wreak havoc on any guests brave enough to attend. And you shouldn't exert yourself. We should cancel and wait for all the repairs to be complete on Fairwilde."

"Come one, come a hundred—a Rundle party must go on. And there is someone I want you all to meet. The Duke of Cheshire."

His stepbrother stretched his long arms and fluffed his starched cravat. "Bully, another wealthy buck to contend with. I thought he wasn't yet out of mourning for his wife's death last autumn."

Theol pitched his countenance toward Lillian. "Surely you are not thinking of a match. She's too young, and I'm sure there are wealthier, more delectable targets to turn the man's head."

Well, at least his stepbrother had some level of decency. Pity it was buried in his twisted values. "Theol is right about our sister being too young. She hasn't even had a season."

Lillian tugged on her silvery, shimmering gloves trimmed with glass beading. The same handiwork matched the beads edging her bodice. A blush tinged her high cheekbones. "Of course not, are you father?"

Lord Rundle pattered over to her and lifted her chin. "No, but he's a good man and supportive of many things about equality. Of judging a man by his character."

A sigh fell from his lips as he pattered back to his seat. "He's become reclusive with our mutual friend, Lord Downing, gone. It's hard to keep good friends."

His stepfather's pale, tired gaze settled Edwin's direction. "He's prefers solitude like you. I want you all to make sure he's entertained and doesn't leave too early. Oh, and the ladies you rescued will be joining us today. The Duchess of

Charming and her companion, Miss Good-mom."

Miss Goodmom? The library started to spin again, but in a good way.

Theol strode to the side bar at the base of a bookshelf and poured himself something from an amber bottle. "Bully, a widow and her spinster friend. I'll leave them to you, stepbrother. They are responsible for your condition."

Rundle swiped at his spectacles and laid them against his pudgy nose. "Yes, leave the lady with fifty thousand a year for Edwin."

"Even at fifty thousand, if it's all the same to you, I'd rather not deal with a widow." Theol's head bounced from Lord Rundle's direction back to Edwin's. "You know how I hate comparisons."

The old man clapped his hands as if he could hardly contain his joy. Well, the man loved gossip. "She's not my friend's widow, but the beneficiary of an unusual degree, as the late duke's title passed straight to her. Charming did something magnanimous for King George, but wasn't fortunate enough to have sons or a near male relation."

"Highly peculiar." Lillian flitted her fan as a rosy glow hit her cheeks. She slipped into the space beside Edwin. "Nonetheless, a woman becoming titled. Positively intriguing."

Theol harrumphed and crossed his arms

against his pristine jet tailcoat and emerald waistcoat. "Well, she does sound attractive, but she's probably stuffy, more so with fifty thousand."

The older woman didn't seem stuffy, but the governess, lovely woman, was someone attainable. The pain to his skull eased a little as his heart ticked up its beat.

Edwin chuckled and caught his stepbrother's gaze. "I don't know, Theol. Rich and stuffy. The duchess is sounding more and more like your love match."

Charlotte stared at the open trunk spilling gowns colored like a soft, muted rainbow. Pinks, lilacs, and gleaming white. She smoothed the silks and satins over her palms as she settled on a pink and white striped one with high ribbons at the bodice.

So lovely, but she tossed the garb back into the trunk. Why was she going to Fairwilde? Tonight wasn't to be her come-out. How could she let the dear old man compel her?

A sigh left her mouth. Lord Rundle looked so fragile when they brought his son to Fairwilde. Then he became insistent about her coming, almost begging. She couldn't help but agree.

She was weak to be swayed by a man, even

a sweet old one, manipulative just like her father.

All the air leached from her lungs. She placed her face atop the cold vanity. When was she supposed to make rules? Would someone else always be in control?

If she were to marry, a husband would own her. What control she had would be gone.

Mercy's squeaky slippers sounded from behind. "Let's see what delight your abigail has picked out for you to wear. Mine chose a high neck…."

Her companion came forward and brushed Charlotte's cheek. "I know you're mad, Duchess, but it's the right thing to do."

Lifting her head, Charlotte jutted her chin out. "I should send you to soiree alone. I couldn't fight your pouting and the dear man." Father's friend looked much older than the last time she saw him at Papa's wake. She shook her head. "The coercion from both of you was too much."

Her friend yanked on the thick muslin sleeves of Charlotte's robe, slipped off the garment, then tightened the ribbons of her corset before slipping a creamy chemise over her head. "We need to inquire about our hero. What better way than at a party?"

"Oh, I don't know. Maybe we could pay him a short visit tomorrow after we purchase those shoes from Ella's." With her thumb, Charlotte slid silver pins along the glass top of her vanity, scattering them with each tinkling hit. "I feel manipulated."

Mercy picked up the striped gown and draped it in Charlotte's lap. "This will look well on you. We'll make your gold curls drape from your chignon. Maybe wear a sapphire choker to bring out your eyes."

"I will send a note to cancel." She sat up, dropping the dress to the floor.

"Too late for that. The Duchess of Charming gave her word. When your father made a promise, it could be counted upon." Mercy scooped up the frock and laid it out on the bed. "Are you not as good as your father?"

Charlotte sank deeper into her chair. All the air sputtered from her lungs as truth rose in her chest. "No. I am not."

Her companion came close and put a hand upon Charlotte's elbow. "Your father was very proud of you. He loved you so. You worry about living up to the great Duke of Charming? Then start by honoring your word and thanking the man who saved our lives."

She took a brush and started sectioning tendrils. "Charlotte, what are you so afraid of? It's not because you didn't get those shoes for your come-out. You may get fixed on certain notions, but you aren't shallow."

"I don't know, but something's wrong." Charlotte reared up and pivoted to the sashed window. Why did the thought of a harmless dinner put knots in her stomach? Prying open the curtains, she witnessed trees bowing to the wind outside. The same foul gusts, which had nearly sent a sign crashing upon her head early, raged outside her safe Grosvenor Square town home.

Leaning on the sill, her heart froze. What if she had died? What would be said of her life?

Nothing of consequence.

She'd be a footnote. The girl with the man's title, dying with no accomplishments other than to have the good fortune of being Lord Charming's daughter. Another point for Papa.

A soft palm clasped her shoulder. "Don't tell me the weather frightens you. I know you too well."

"At my age, twenty-one, Father had already taken three world tours and set up missionaries in Ireland. What will be my contribution to the world? Will it be to marry a peer and produce a proper heir?"

"Lineage is important. No man can bring a child to life. That's something that only God can do through a woman."

"My father got special permission for me to keep his title. Shouldn't I use it to do something of meaning? Before today, I was consumed with finding the perfect shoes. We only remained in Cheapside to ply the owner for those special slippers."

"Pretty, gauzy things." Mercy's voice was lyrical. "With the right amount of heel height, you'll have such appeal."

"You're not listening." Charlotte hugged her simple friend. Maybe Mercy was right; she shouldn't think so much upon this. Who could choose their destiny absent God? *Father of Heaven, will you help?*

Silence. Nothing but the howl of the wind. "Augh."

Nestling Charlotte's jaw with her chubby palm, Mercy guided her toward the mirror. "You fret too much, but if we need to do more, we simply need to try. What about one of the duke's causes?"

Charlotte sank into her reading chair, kicking her feet out. "Papa always had a plan for me. He chose the families I was to be friends with. What languages I was to be educated in. He chose my schedule. Everything. And he was planning a match with one of the Theols."

"Now, before you fret yourself into a marriage, let's get you dressed." Mercy tugged a silver comb through Charlotte's rumpled curls.

Soon bright-gold tendrils hung everywhere. Charlotte couldn't see anything but the candlelight reflecting from the vanity's mirror.

"Dearest, just because your father suggested it doesn't make it bad."

"Nor does it make it right for me." Her stomach refused to unclench. The duke's heavy-handedness in everything sometimes made it challenging to like her father.

But she did miss him, the certitude that flowed from his fingers, dripped in his every action and cadence. How could he always be so certain of everything? "Do we have to stay through dinner? Fairwilde parties go on quite late. I remember once Papa didn't come home until two in the morning."

"Then let's make a pact. No matter how much fun we are having, we will leave by midnight before the church bell strikes all twelve gongs."

Blowing a lock from her face, almost modeling the whistle of the harsh wind, Charlotte cleared hair from her eyes. "By twelve, no later."

"Very good." Mercy leaned over to grip a piece of silver ribbon, squashing Charlotte beneath the woman's heavyset figure. "Cheer up. All your father's judgments couldn't be bad. He chose me to be with you."

When her companion stepped back and Charlotte could breathe, she nodded. Mercy was a good friend, very loyal. "I just want to choose. From now on, I, the Duchess of Charming, will have the final say."

"Of course, sweetheart. By midnight we will be to home in Grosvenor Square." Mercy shrouded her in a hug. "From then on, you can do whatever you want."

There was no use fighting. To thank her hero, Charlotte would go and smile, then count the seconds to leave. No one understood her. No one ever could.

Edwin steadied himself at the top of Fairwilde's main staircase, gripping a waxy knurled post. The place sparkled. Even the old marble tiles below gleamed. Mama would be proud.

Yet, butterflies danced in his gut. Formal dinners meant dancing, remembering which fork to start with, and a hundred other rituals of the *ton*.

His fingers tightened on the post, sending a fresh wave of pain to his temples. He loosened his hold and took a deep breath. He'd have to get used to society, being a part of it as he was. In another few years, his sister would be of age, ready for a season.

To protect her interests from Theol's suspected motives or the lax of a mite-too-doting father, she'd need someone with a level head to help her make a wise choice. Not everyone could be blessed like their mother, to gain the love of two respectable men.

Lillian pranced to the foot of the stairs and

craned her neck toward him. "You haven't changed your mind? You are staying?"

With a slow nod of his head, he started his descent down the carpeted stairs. What he wouldn't give for this day to be over. He took his time lowering himself down each step, forging a rhythm: wince, breathe, next footfall, repeat. "I'm coming."

With her watery towels and Abraham's flavored-ice bundles, their treatments reduced Edwin's pain to a dull ache at the back of his noggin.

Lillian lifted her palm to him. "Papa nearly burst with joy when you said you'd stay and not go to your town home and mope."

Stars twinkled in Lillian's eyes as Edwin powered to the last treads. He gripped her hand. "I aim to please."

"You will enjoy yourself, Brother."

"Wait—don't increase my bill. I only promised to remain upright, nothing about fun."

A smile lit her oval face. Her lashes fluttered. "Kidder."

The girl was a charmer, and he'd make everyone but himself happy tonight. What type of role model would he be if he let ringing ears set him down and disappointed her and Lord Rundle? "Lead on."

Arm in arm, they made the short walk to the drawing room's doors. The strings of a violin wrapped a melody about him, lessening the sting of moving. Could he rest in the doorway?

Lillian whipped out her fan as she looked out at the milling crowd. "Pretty nice turnout for such foul weather. You never know. You might just find my future sister-in-law tonight." She glanced sidelong at him. "Mr. and Mrs. Edwin Cinder. It does sound well. And I would so like a sister."

Find a wife? Another thing he hadn't promised to do tonight. A sigh steamed out as his mind drifted to the lady with the bluest eyes. The first woman of the right station to catch his interest in a long time, and he had to pass out at her feet. What must she think of him? What would he say to the duchess's pretty companion tonight?

Lillian reached up and tweaked his cravat. "Thank you for not fussing too much with Shelby." Lillian's light blue eyes clouded, and she fingered the glass beads trimming her silver glove. "I tried to hide the brandy, but he still found it."

A little piece of Edwin's heart shriveled at the concern warbling in her soft voice. "Don't fret about your brother. In fact, don't fret about anything tonight. Now, go be the best hostess for Lord Rundle."

She patted his arm and pivoted. "Don't blow away. I must check on Papa. He's moving slower these days." Her smile dimmed before she traipsed into to the room.

A few early guests bowed and stopped her. Soon his sister disappeared behind twittering fans.

His gaze fell upon the freshly chalked floor. The musicians began to set up again. He took a step backward, then another, and another, until he leaned against the Grecian column in the quiet hall.

Free of dancing dangers, he filled his chest. Love for the grand arches of Fairwilde Manor warmed his insides. If he hadn't needed to take over the shoe trade for his father, Edwin might've tried building things. Yes, studying architecture. That would've been nice.

For a moment, he shut his lids and imagined bold curves formed in cut limestone, but the sketches evaporated, turning into patterns for soles and new tassels for boots.

Hot air pushed out his lips. Too much cobbler in his blood, not enough dreamer.

"The air is better in here." A tall man of dark-colored hair neared. Judging by the lift of his head and the elegant twists of his necktie, he must be a gentleman of some rank.

Searching for a properly worded response, Edwin squared his shoulders. "It is better than being in the wind storm or the crowded drawing room. I am Cinder."

"Yes, I know. You provided the shoes for a charity of my good friend, the late Lord Charming. I am Cheshire."

This must be the duke Lord Rundle discussed. "I'm just doing a small part. From what I hear, it's you and Lord Charming who funded the greater good, the teachers, the shelters, the clothing."

"Everything counts." Though Cheshire smiled, shadows hung about his eyes. Something troubled him, but what could trouble a duke?

Cheshire cleared his throat. "The big is made up of lots of small. A wise man values all contributions no matter the weight, and makes the time to honor them. Tomorrow isn't promised."

Yes. One never knows when a sign will drop. "I'll remember that."

"Rundle also said you were injured saving my friend's daughter. Your eyes are bloodshot. Shouldn't you be resting?"

"I'll suffer through. My small contribution to Rundle's joy. He loves entertaining and couldn't even wait for the workmen to finish their renovation to the brickwork."

"I saw the scaffolding. Hopefully they did enough reappointing of the mortar to keep all the bricks in place. A slovenly job could be dangerous..." Cheshire craned his head from side to side. "Especially in a windstorm. I'm glad I left my sweet daughter in the country."

"Oh, Duke." The high-pitched wail sent a shiver up Edwin's spine, making his ears hurt.

Cheshire's face pinched as if he'd failed in hide and seek.

A woman with rouged cheeks, fair complexion, and curly auburn hair plodded close and looped her arm about the duke's. "If I didn't know any better, I'd think you were avoiding me."

"Cinder, this is my cousin, Miss Margaret Smythe."

"Good to meet you, ma'am." Edwin bent, lowering his head a little. Hopefully, his small dip was enough to convey welcome.

"Pleased as well." She nodded, then slipped between them, putting her back to Edwin. "Duke, how am I to protect you from unwelcome attention if you run from me? You've been widowed six months. You're a prime target for every match-making mother here."

"Yes, with you hovering about, no one will dare intrude." Cheshire's lips flattened to a line. The duke seemed pained. Yet, it was unclear the cause: the widowhood, the match-making mothers, or the smitten cousin.

Prying at her hands, Cheshire freed himself. "Miss Smythe, I will be along in few minutes. Save me a spot on your dance card."

Her cheery expression darkened. "Anything you wish, my lord." Swishing her pink train, the lady pattered back to the drawing room.

The duke wrenched his neck. "Lord Rundle says you struggle with finding your footing in these settings. Trust me. Except for my daughter, I'd turn back to the time when my ascension as my uncle's heir was a lesser possibility. Then people knew my name, William St. Landon, not just my rank."

Lord Rundle had noticed Edwin's unease and mentioned it to the duke. Why would he? Embarrassed, Edwin's hands fisted behind his back. "That's an easy platitude for you, a gentleman by birth."

"A good character is welcome at any table, not just the ones he purchases." The duke turned and headed back into the crowd.

Self-conscious, Edwin retreated and headed for the stairs. The guest room he had reclined in would be a perfect place to hide.

He lifted his head. *No.* No running, not for a Cinder. He turned and leaned against the stair rail. He wouldn't slight Lord Rundle, even if he bandied Edwin's name with his friends.

Dipping into his pocket, he pulled out his watch. Straining, he attempted to read the tiny hands. Maybe it said 8:15. His close vision remained impaired. It didn't matter; he'd withstand. A good night of sleep should make his eyesight crystal clear again, like the crystal-line blue eyes of the young lady he'd rescued.

The muffled introduction of the Duchess of Charming filtered into the air. His pulse ticked up. He lifted his gaze to catch sight of the woman, but more so her companion. Nothing but blurs filled his vision. The whispers of people pouring into the drawing room blended with the festive music seeping into the hall.

Abraham waved a cup of negus under Edwin's nose. "You look a bit glassy, sir. I think you should find a bed."

Not yet, not without another look at the companion—if she came. Edwin shrugged as he took a cup and sipped the tangy liquid. "You're a wise man, but I'll retire as everyone sits down to dinner." That would be enough time to find her, or put Lillian on the task. He set the cup back on Abraham's tray.

The door to the orangery at the end of the hall blasted open. Two footmen came running and pressed it closed. The storm must be growing worse.

"Excuse me, Mr. Cinder. I'm going to put more grooms on all the doors. Can't have a breeze extinguishing candelabras or cooling the soup." The elegant man marched away.

What wind could withstand Abraham? No one was a match for the dutiful man's regimen.

More guests entered Fairwilde. Probably

party goers who'd ridden too far to turn back. Soon people spilled from the drawing room into the hall. The quiet evaporated. Smiling ladies appeared everywhere.

They moved a little fast for his eyes to discern a recognizable face, so Edwin looked down, spying their shoes and counting the one's purchased from one of his Ella stores.

The shape and color of his designs, he knew by heart. Perhaps, it was best to avoid direct eye contact. Catching someone's attention could lead to dancing. It was best to avoid such while wobbly. Well, he wasn't so great without a headache, either. Edwin was patient. If he didn't stumble upon the miss of interest tonight, he'd see her tomorrow at Ella's, his domain.

The seven chimes of a long case clock sounded at the pause in the music. Dinner would soon be served, and no clear blues had found him. Well, he hadn't moved much from his spot in the hall either. Tomorrow, he'd see the young lady or ply Lord Rundle to make it happen.

He turned to advance to a guest bedchamber and caught a glimpse of lilac slippers. They weren't one of his designs with such simple lacy bows, but the shoes were elegant.

The fine satin didn't move from him and stayed opposite his dark footwear.

Slowly, he lifted his gaze. The lady's brilliant golden curls reflected candlelight. Blue eyes, bluer than a pure mountain spring, burned a hole through his soul. Was this the goddess from Cheapside, now shed of her black attire?

It was she. His pulse raced as she took a step closer. He absorbed the proud lift of her chin, cute button nose, and endless gold lashes. Where was Lord Rundle? He needed his step-father to make a proper introduction to the angel.

Charlotte had spent enough time mingling and was about to beckon a footman for her wrap, when she spotted her hero in the shadows of the hall. Now she stood next to her handsome rescuer, waiting for him to greet her. Maybe he didn't recognize her.

She lifted her arm, holding out her palm to him. "Sir?"

The man never claimed her fingers but bowed. He seemed almost shy as he stood erect, gripping his ear.

She cocked her head, taking in the reluctant tall form. His autumn-brown eyes were darker, sadder than before. "Are you well?"

He started to nod, but stopped. "I am." His voice sounded muted but pleasant.

"Not one to run on?" Smiling, she tried to coax him into conversation. It should be easy.

All the men of the *ton* wished for her attention, not that she wanted to give it. "Then let me express how grateful I am. You risked your life—"

"Ma'am, I am sure that anybody..." He bit his lip. "Anyone would do the same."

First, his mouth curled up, then his gaze met hers. The intensity rippled through her. Her pulse raced in time to the quickened strings of the harp music tickling her ear. He looked away. Was there something on the floor of interest?

She peered too but saw nothing but polished planks and the edge of a golden tapestry leading to the stairs. When his calf-skinned slippers with dulled buckles edged away, she caught his arm. "Sir, I know we've not been properly introduced, but sometimes, one must go against formalities. Don't retreat; give me the opportunity to thank you."

This time his hand covered her palm. Through his white gloves and hers, she could feel his raw strength. "I don't retreat, but I make wise choices of my battles."

A dimple showed on his lean cheek. "Besides, there is nothing owed. Nothing at all."

A flush heated her neck and soon made its way to her face. Maybe one didn't need a bunch of words. Useless vowels and consonants. Why use any, if a man could offer one look and make her blush like a wallflower?

He released her, letting her fingers float to her side. "Enjoy the party. Think nothing more of the bad… unpleasant incident."

Before the urge to babble took control of her tongue, she reached for his sleeve, her thumb slipping along the fine wool, tracing the muscles underneath. "Stand up with me."

A puzzled look crossed his countenance, his lips thinning to a line. "Dancing? Shouldn't the man do the asking and only after a proper introduction? Is this a new rule of etiquette?"

"Yes, if said man gets clunked on the head for a lady." She whipped her wide fan, stirring the humid air. A hint of barberry, like a sweet ice, kissed her nose. He smelled delicious.

Using her silken fan as a means for privacy, she whispered, "It won't hurt. Nothing like the sign."

Her hero seemed to hesitate, shifting his weight.

Was he nervous or shy? How delightful, better than cake with mounds of snowy bliss icing. She, a female, took the opportunity to pursue. For now she'd avoid the niggling thought in her brain that her father might be right about a match to the Theols. "You won't refuse a lady's request?"

"A reel, aye?" He took her palm within his. "I may not be the steadiest, and I hope not to embarrass you."

She led him to the drawing room, where couples had lined up for the next set. One violinist followed by another crafted a fast tune.

Smiling, she set up opposite him. Locking hands, he spun her in the steps. His hold exuded strength, not limp-wristed or weak in his fingers.

Trading places, they looped around with the couple next to them, then moved on. Her hero wasn't bad, though she wished he'd look up more. Was he counting his steps? The son of an earl should be born with these movements ingrained. Well, he must have better pursuits with his time.

She caught his gaze, and her lips lifted into a bigger smile.

He went the wrong direction, but he swirled and corrected. His cheeks grew redder.

Could such a simple gesture have made him off-balanced? Maybe all men needed to be hit with a falling sign to lose their bluster.

Half into the set, he stopped. "Enough torture." The words were a whisper, but loud enough for her to hear.

"This can be exhausting." She wasn't tired but knew it would be better to appear as if she needed a rest. Taking his arm, she followed him from the center of the chalked floor to the chairs along the wall.

A young girl with pale blue eyes came up to

them. "I can't believe you danced, brother. You almost never dance. Oh, miss, you are always welcome to all of my father's parties."

Beads jiggled on her shiny glove as his sister whipped out her fan and swatted him on the arm before scampering back into the crush of guests.

Her hero smiled, then winced. He must be suffering.

"You should sit. You could have told me you weren't well."

"I'm not one to complain. And you are very insistent." He eased into a chair. His motion was slow, almost as if he visualized a proper way to sit. "I do like a lady who knows what she wants."

Her face flamed again. She bent and looked into his large eyes. Thick, long lashes hovered over the rich brown irises.

He blinked heavily until she stepped back.

"Your close vision is pained? My father was like that when he lost his glasses. We could've stopped sooner."

A man of medium height and with a long crooked nose came close, scowling with each step. "Shoemaker? Couldn't finish a set? Maybe the saint is human."

"Shoemaker?" What an odd nickname. She gazed at her seated hero with his eyes rolling up. The onlooker must be an annoyance. "You shouldn't have to endure the loud music or other bothers."

"Yes, Duchess. I tried to make him leave." The man hiccupped. The smell of alcohol surrounded his words. "He stays where he's not wanted."

Her shy hero rose. "Duchess?"

She pivoted from the bewildered expression scrunching the handsome man's face to the inebriated one. "Why would one of Lord Rundle's sons not be wanted at his own father's party?"

"Is that what he told you? He's not a son. Cinder's a stepson, one who peddles shoes for a living. A merchant." He poked a finger into her hero's chest. "My, my, saint. Now you're a liar."

Questions singed her brow. Charlotte turned to her shy dance partner. "You're not a Theol?"

A deep sigh left his mouth. "This is a mistake. It's the reason we need proper introductions." He bowed and sidestepped her.

The loud man's hiccups and chuckles became deafening. "Cinder, the slipper man."

Cinder as in Cinder's Ella, the best place in London for shoes? The owner of the shoes she had to have. With her fan, she hooked her hero's shoulder, stopping him. "Wait. I need an explanation."

Fists clenching, he turned back. The heavy

beating of his heart could be heard above the lulling of the musician's set. "Ma'am, you're looking for a nobleman's son. Lord Theol, the drunk, is behind you."

CHAPTER THREE

The Grand Party

dwin turned from the couple, Beauty and the Beast, and squeezed between nosy onlookers. His cheeks surely burnt off his face and fell to the floor.

His heart squeezed, almost slipping between his ribs when he caught Lord Rundle's gaze. Never, ever did he want to cause the man embarrassment.

The old fellow smiled and motioned with his finger to lift Edwin's chin.

That was too much to accomplish with his pride falling into his shoes. With a final glimpse, he witnessed the duchess's lovely figure traipsing around the baron. Perhaps his stepbrother's rich chatter was no better than a tradesman's.

Part of him wanted to go to her and say something to clear the air, but this wasn't a battle worth fighting. The determined young duchess was out of a cobbler's reach. Shaking his head, Edwin continued his march underneath the shaking grand chandelier in the center of the room. The wavering lights, his dear mother's signature handiwork, illuminated a path of retreat. The tension in his shoulders increased as the musicians started up again.

A few fans waved at him, but no more dancing tonight. And none of them were prettier than the duchess.

He spied her again by the punch bowl. Lean neck, slender build. She was a graceful woman. Though his vision hadn't fully cleared, he knew it was her. He could feel her gaze boring through him.

Well, for a few minutes, having those blue eyes to himself meant the world.

At a pace just shy of a run, he quickened his steps. He didn't stop until he'd fled the drawing room and stood again in the long hall.

Oh, why couldn't such loveliness belong to a merchant's daughter? Someone he'd have a chance of winning, —not that he wanted to marry. There was too much to do, like keeping his stepfather from overspending, influencing Lillian's prospects, potentially opening another Ella's in the bazaar at Mayfield. Yes, too much work to do maintaining Mother's dreams than to find wedded bliss.

He posted himself at his column, leaning his noggin against the cold marble. With less people in the hall, Edwin could breathe. His posture sagged before he bolted upright. Someone would bother Lord Rundle about his stepson's ill-bred behavior. It was time to escape. What was the best way to leave?

A footman stood watch over the orangery door. The poor fellow pushed hard against it, as if the thing would burst open if he moved.

Well, with a liveried guard, the orangery wasn't the best route, and the weather looked worse.

Maybe to bed. The guest room he'd refreshed in earlier? Yes. That would do.

Pivoting toward the steps, he rammed into Abraham.

"Whoa there, Mr. Cinder." The quick butler caught the silver cups sliding across his gleaming tray. Not a one hit the ground. This man knew how not to make a fool of himself.

"In a mighty hurry. Still feeling poorly?" Concern laced the deep voice.

"Very poorly." *Embarrassed myself with a duchess.* Edwin tugged on his cravat as if it choked. Right now anything having to do with starch and finery did. "How are you always so ordered? You maintain such poise."

Abraham stopped positioning his goblets, not quite finishing their alignment into a perfect circle on his tray. "Much like you when they come into one of your shops."

He lifted his gaze to meet Edwin's. Deep chocolate eyes full of wisdom beamed at him. "I treat them with respect and let the fruit of my deeds speak for me."

Yet, customers in Ella's were in Edwin's domain. He was lord and master of the lasting operations, the sole constructions. He chose the fabrics, the final embellishments. And the *ton*—all shoppers—respected him there. None belittled him.

Or insinuated that he lied.

"I think I might go to my residence in Cheapside... where I belong."

The butler shook his head. "The weather's become increasingly foul. You'll need to wait 'til this wind dies down. It's more brutal than before. You'd think the roof would blow off."

Willing his hands not to ball into fists, Edwin lowered his head. "I just need to be away from everyone."

"Your mother would get like that, too. The late countess found solace with her Bible in the library. Give it a try? The fire's still goin'. Poke it a bit to keep things lit. I'll bring you some hot tea and a spoon of honey."

Mother's library? Quiet, full of calming memories of her. "Make it a big spoon, Abraham. Yes, I'll rest there for another hour. Then leave."

Nodding, Edwin plodded the final distance to the room, opened the door, and slipped inside.

Abraham was right. The hearth still burned. The place felt toasty, more so than before. Maybe the butler knew Edwin would end up here, alone licking his wounds.

With a shake of his head, he trudged forward narrowing his gaze onto the sturdy sofa, the comfortable, overstuffed thing. It possessed the correct amount of height so his long legs didn't cramp sitting upon it. The padding was stiff, solid, and right now the most inviting place in the world.

Looking past the high walls of books, he glimpsed Mother's mahogany desk. How many times had he come to Fairwilde and spied her here, preparing correspondences or reading?

The sounds of the drawing room's pianoforte echoed. The heavy whistle of the wind soon took over. He closed his eyes and remembered his mother's cheery laughter. How did the brave woman find her way, straddling both worlds: the rich set and the working classes?

Even in her final year, beset with stomach ailments, she visited each of the Ella's stores regularly, knew the names of all the clerks. She spent her last day hosting a Rundle party. Well, who would miss a Rundle party?

Chuckling, Edwin eased onto the sofa and laid his head back. Maybe if he wished hard enough, he'd start this day over. This time he'd stay in bed in his town home and send his man-of-all-work from Cheapside with a note to his stepfather's begging off. With his head still ringing, he'd pretend someone else risked all to rescue a duchess. And that person was still dancing with her, enjoying her smiles.

Charlotte drank another cup of the negus punch. The tart liquid wet the knots lodged in her stomach. Her hero stormed off without an explanation and left her with a drunk. A sharp-nosed, sharp-tongued drunk.

If Mercy hadn't blocked him, she'd still be trapped talking with the lout. She took another sip, but almost dropped the goblet.

Oh, no. The drunk had trailed her to the refreshments table.

Lord Theol waved his quizzing glass at her. "Close your mouth, dear. Flies will gather." He held his hand to her. "Now that we don't have an audience, let me show you how a reel should be done. That will smooth over this t...tiff."

The man hiccupped. His gaze wandered over her, making her want to bunch up the neckline of her lilac gown. She almost wished she were still covered head to toe in dark mourning garb.

"Sir, I don't feel like dancing, but I'm sure that some young lady would relish your attention." Someone as daft as he, no doubt.

He reached out and gripped her hand. "I think you would enjoy a turn about the chalked floor with an expert, one knowledgeable in these affairs."

Charlotte popped out her fan and swatted his fingers.

It was a hard crack that made him rear back with reddened knuckles.

She lifted her head high and proceeded through the crowd toward the pianoforte in the corner of the large drawing room. The pompous baron didn't follow this time. There was no way he and her hero could be related, at least not by blood.

Mercy came over to her, sipping from a shiny silver cup, dribbles slipping down her chin. "Duchess, you do know how to enliven a party. See, you needed practice before the court presentation at week's end."

Barely keeping her eyes from rolling, Charlotte grimaced and flitted her fan.

Her companion giggled again. "Just a note. Don't have men fighting over you all at once, and never indoors. The queen won't take kindly to anyone outdoing—"

Charlotte put a hand to her friend's lips.

"Shhh. They weren't fighting over me. I think I was just caught in the middle of their argument."

With a wiggle, Mercy shook her head, then loud-slurped her negus. "Our rescuer is the rich Mr. Cinder. We were at his shop in Cheapside. He's Lord Rundle's stepson from his late countess, Ella Theol. Maybe if you dance with him again, you could get the *handsome* man to give you those shoes."

"He wasn't that handsome."

"Oh yes he was." Mercy giggled.

Charlotte's cheeks felt hot as she remembered their hero's large autumn-gold eyes and perfect nose. "And riches aren't everything."

"Well, not for you. Your father provided very well for you, but you shouldn't overlook a gentleman because he doesn't need your money."

"I'm not sure he's a gentleman. Lord Theol said Mr. Cinder was a merchant." Was that why her hero almost refused her invitation to dance? Was it why he was so careful in his steps?

"Maybe not a gentleman by birth. But anyone who would risk injury to save you is a gentleman in my heart. And since he's a stepson, he's not a Theol. You said you didn't want one."

Between his headache and the argument with the baron, she'd led him into more pain.

"True, but I think I offended him."

"According to his sister, he had quite an ache when he awoke, but he's struggling through the party for his stepfather. Mr. Cinder's quite fond of Lord Rundle. Our hero is brave and kind to his relations." Mercy plucked at the side of the cup. The pitch sounded like a Christmas bell. "Quite a young man even if he's *just a merchant*. Unless something better comes along—"

"Mercy, stop. No more ordering of my life." Tugging on her sleeves, Charlotte straightened her shoulders and stepped around her companion. "I have an apology to tender."

She wandered past the thick groves of guests to return to the hall where she'd first spied the reluctant man. Except for a groom posted at a door, it was vacant. No hero.

The wind beat on the panes of glass, rattling everything. A shiver swept down her spine as she heard the creaking noise of the hinges, so similar to the screeching sounds of the chains before they snapped.

She swallowed her fright when the butler advanced. He carried a set of plates. It must be time to serve dinner, but food was the last thing on Charlotte's mind. Righting a slight was the top priority.

"This side of the house isn't for guests, ma'am. Lord Rundle is still making repairs." He stood to attention and held the heavy-looking tray with one hand. His head cocked to the side. "Might I help?"

"I'm looking for..." What was his name? It wasn't Rundle. She felt her foot tapping as if the energy would jog her memory. "I'm looking for Lord Rundle's stepson."

Wise eyes widened as his sturdy wal-nut-colored chin nodded. "Mr. Cinder is in the library. Down the hall and through the door, miss."

"Thank you." Charlotte picked up her skirts and paced to the room. Her insides churned, but she wouldn't let her nerves show.

A small glow filtered under the door, and the scent of burnt hickory followed. She thought about knocking, but that seemed timid. Her father wouldn't have knocked, even if he were in the wrong. Filling her lungs, she turned the glass knob and opened the door.

The room was dark save one candle on the wall sconce and the flames of the hearth. Yet, even in the dim light, the magnificence of the library could not be missed. Each wall was cov-ered with endless shelves, each holding all manner of leather spines or an occasional Dres-den figurine.

Why didn't Lord Rundle incorporate this beauty into the crowded party flow? Oh, the butler did say repairs were being made.

She lifted her head and moved inside. Though logs burned in the hearth, her arms pimpled as if the storm air had found its way inside. Wishing she'd kept her shawl, she rubbed her short sleeves and turned toward the window. The easy breeze that had rumpled her skirts and wrinkled Mercy's cape as they descended from the carriage was no more. The violent winds lifted twigs and leaves, slamming them against the glass.

This was not a night to be out: not for shoes, not for a trial come-out, not for insulting an honest man.

A dark lump, a large body, reclined on the sofa. Mr. Cinder?

In case it wasn't, she tiptoed around the sofa and cast her gaze upon him.

Young, handsome, sleeping. It was her brooding hero with a book—maybe a Bible—on his lap and a spoon dangling from his lips.

A chuckle almost slipped from her mouth. Was there a playful streak, hidden within the strong vessel? When a soft snore made the spoon vibrate and slip to the side, she clamped her teeth. He looked almost innocent. Perhaps, beneath the toughened exterior was something soft, vulnerable. Something a willful woman could draw out.

She shook her head. Her appearance was to offer an apology. Nothing more. Yet, what was the best way to wake him, and cause the least amount of alarm? Vague thoughts of how the sleeping princess Briar Rose from the fairy tale was awakened speared Charlotte's thoughts. Now her skin felt hot. Her palms became damp within her gloves. She stretched her fingers, and before her resolve gave way, she cleared her throat.

His eyes blinked and a small smile bloomed before his countenance blanked. Was he happy to see her?

He sat up, stuffed the spoon in his pocket, then folded his arms. "Yes, Duchess?" His tone was stiff, off-pitch, maybe from wrestling sleep or being caught with silverware in his mouth.

Her tongue felt heavy, but she took a deep breath and blurted, "Sorry."

A dimple showed, then disappeared in the strong plains of his jaw. "To what do I owe—what is the right word?—such pity?"

Oh, he wasn't going to make this easy. She lifted her head and focused on the books, not the way the flame's reflection danced in his large eyes. "I made an assumption and that caused a problem, a nasty disagreement. I apologize."

"Well, thank you." He closed his eyes and settled back against the heavy, tufted couch. "Now go back to the party where you belong."

"What?" Her gaze lingered on his face. How

could that strong jaw conjure words of dismissal, with no more feeling than she did waiting for a carriage? "Sir, why are you so short with me?"

"The public party's in the drawing room. This is a private library." He pointed over his head toward the door.

Another man telling her *no*. Fury swelled in her chest. She steadied her palm against the ribbons adorning her bodice. "You are dismissing me, and with such little civility."

His shoulders shrugged, but he kept his lids shut. "Yes, Duchess, I am."

She was not a little girl waiting for her father's attention. She was grown—a duchess, nonetheless. "Why are you being so ungracious, so pigheaded?"

"Outside this room, my mother's library, I will bow and scrape, pay attention to the etiquette and manners you genteels crave, but in here I am simply Edwin Cinder." He patted the leather tome resting on the thick curve of his knee. "An equal to anyone. I have son-ship where it counts the most."

She folded her arms. He was right, but she wouldn't let him intimidate her and send her scurrying from the room like some weak creature. "You can at least look at me. Son-ship should have manners."

The room groaned as he stood to his feet.

He plodded the two steps separating them. "A brave duchess, to confront a man, alone in a library. What of your reputation conversing with a tradesman?"

Why was he intentionally baiting her? "You wouldn't dare do anything untoward. Like my father, I am a quick judge of people. A man who nearly died trying to save my life would hardly try to ruin it."

"I suppose there is something to your logic. Well, apology accepted. Conscience clean. You can leave me now, Duchess."

Her feet locked to the floor at the indifferent air of his tone. "Well, now that is done. You can oblige me with one more thing?"

His brow rose. "And that would be?"

"Sell me the slippers you have on display. I must have the ones with the lace at Cinder's Ella in Cheapside."

A chuckle escaped his mouth. "My, you are fired up over them, even while falsely apologizing, but they're not for sale. The price is too high for you."

"What? I can pay anything. They match almost perfectly to my dress."

He rubbed his temples, then bent as if to ensure she'd not miss his rejection. "An Ella creation, almost perfect? You are mistaken. They are always perfect."

"My court dress has pearls, yards and

yards, not crystals, but those slippers will do. I wish to wear them to see the queen." She put a hand to her hip and straightened her shoulders. "Is there a better cause? You'd rather they'd be perched in glass and forgotten?"

His lips pursed as he straightened. "The price for those shoes is a heart. Well more like two. I made them for my mother to attest my love and support for her. She wore them for her wedding to Lord Rundle, where she gave her own heart in support of all his dreams."

Something in her chest lifted at the sound of his voice, the passion and emotion woven in each word. When had someone wanted to support her dreams? Mercy and Papa loved her, but they followed the same script of low expectations given to all females: *Marry well*.

Almost breathless, her voice diminished to a whisper. "That is a high price to pay."

A blast of air hit her temples as if the ceiling lifted, letting in the storm. The harsh noise hurt her ears. Were the party guests coming closer to the library? She gazed back toward her hero.

His simmering eyes scanned from side to side. His head moved above hers. Was he looking for another way to say no? She fully comprehended his meaning, and her lobes stung at how shallow her reasoning sounded.

"Duchess." His face paled as the sound grew deafening. "Remember, I'd never hurt you!"

Her heart pounded as he grabbed her, pulling her close.

She pushed with all her might to free herself from his iron grip as the roof fell in on them.

CHAPTER FOUR

Trapped

fter several minutes of Fairwilde's groaning, the horrible noises of breaking timbers and exploding glass ended. A last rush of dust dumped upon Charlotte's nostrils. The scent of split oak and musty paper stung her tongue, smothering her screams with coughs.

Something dull and heavy fell, smiting her chest and pushed out the little air trapped within her lungs. With her free arm, she slapped the book from her chin. Her skin pimpled as blackness sank into her brain. Why would this happen? How could she be trapped beneath a mound of rubble?

Keep your wits, Charlotte.

Her ears rang, sounding of her father's voice, his admonition, as he taught her to ride. *Be strong, my girl.*

The man ate calm with his crumpets. His

daughter should embody it, too. She wiggled her toes. Though something heavy pinned her legs, she could move her feet. Maybe things would end well.

Smelling tart ink, she lifted her hand and pushed against the blackness. Her fingers might've stretched ten or twelve inches before hitting a solid object. She struck it again, her nails hitting wood, an unmovable beam. Imprisoned beneath the rafter. She swallowed the tears filling her throat. "God, how do I get free?"

The dark world above howled as the unnatural wind raged again. Creaking and shaking, the hovel was on the verge of collapse. The vicious storm wouldn't be over until it killed her.

She screamed, but her breaths became shallow. Pressing her lips together, she closed her eyes. Maybe there wasn't enough air. What if this pocket collapsed, too? Would her last moments be spent alone?

Trembles coursed every inch of her. She blinked and shouted and yelled some more, but no one came. Maybe no one could. Had Fairwilde's collapse killed everyone in the ballroom? What of her friend, her poor Mercy?

Fear grew from Charlotte's cold toes and raced to her bosom. It fisted about her heart as if to wring out all its life. This wasn't fair. She hadn't yet lived, and now everything would be gone. Panting, she rocked from side to side and kicked her feet until she kneed something. It was large and solid, but not like a rafter beam. No, this seemed human.

Images of dancing with Mr. Cinder spun in her head, of him pulling her tight into his arms as Fairwilde crashed down upon them. Expectation stirred inside. She had to know for sure. Unable to see more than an inch in front of her, she reached out until her thumb stroked heavy woolen fabric. Mr. Cinder's tailcoat? Splaying her fingers, she clutched a shoulder. It had to be him draped across her abdomen, not moving.

She shivered from the thought of not being alone and that the fellow who'd saved her life twice might be severely injured…or might have been killed from the falling house. A dead man could be caught on her limbs!

Her lungs stopped working. Tears dribbled down Charlotte's cheeks. She had to know if her hero was alive, or if she could help him. Tentatively at first, then with more confidence, she reached out into the darkness until her palms landed on his arm.

Thick and well-muscled, she gripped it, then slipped her hand against his shoulder, tracing its dip to his neck. She smoothed his square chin. "Mr. Cinder?"

Straddled along her side with an arm and leg thrust across her, he didn't answer. His skin felt cold but a pulse pounded along his throat. Life still pumped in his veins, but for how long?

She opened her mouth, but only a whimper released, garbling her words. "Please... wake up."

The wind moaned, then quieted. Icy silence surrounded them.

No noise of people picking through bricks. No expectation of getting medical attention for Mr. Cinder. No glimmer of hope for rescue. None at all.

"God, are you there? Is this it? Did you not have more plans for me?" Her windpipe constricted as it filled with a sob. "Answer me, please."

The dull thumping of her heart reached her ears, nothing else. God must not be there. Perhaps He didn't believe a duke's daughter had need of anything, but Charlotte did. Desperate to be filled with the peace Papa possessed before his eyes shut forever, she cried anew. Hot, wet drops sank onto her cheeks. Though her father was gone, she still desired his protection and care.

Mr. Cinder shifted. "I'm here."

She mopped at her face. He was alive and conscious. "Mr. Cin—"

His arm stiffened and locked about her waist. The bones of his jawline flattened against her stomach.

Her newfound joy turned to confusion. Confined in this tight spot so close to a man, Charlotte felt her damp face smolder. This pocket under the rubble fitted like a coffin, forcing her hero against her. Lying so near was intimate and scary. The thudding of his heart vibrated through her.

Too fearful of her father, no man had ever been so forward as to hug her or seek a kiss. Now one lay close to her. Waves of loneliness cresting in her mind receded. She let her fingers find his skull and sweep into his hair. What would become of them?

Something brushed Edwin's face. He shook his head and sought to return to his dream: the curves of the Taj Mahal, a place he'd love to study if work relented. As he tried to adjust his stubborn pillow, silk brushed his cheek.

His bed had linens. This wasn't his home. Had he gotten drunk and wandered into one of Theol's brothels? Edwin's pulse raced. He bolted up and slammed his skull.

Only a few inches of clearance overhead? A coffin? He'd heard horrible tales of being buried alive. Panic thundered his heart.

"Mr. Cinder. You're awake."

He gulped air with his mouth. Had he taken one hit too many? Surely, he had. Two buried in the grave. He pitched and rocked and found a bit more room in the jet-blackness. The urge to live burned in his lungs.

Groping fingers touched his cheek. "Sir, answer me. Are you very much injured?"

He swept his hands, sieving through the darkness until he caught a satiny palm. A woman's glove. He brought their union to his chest. The memory of protecting a beautiful lady from Fairwilde's falling walls lit his mind. "Duchess?"

"Yes." The low sound originated from underneath him.

Oh, goodness. He straddled her. She must think him an oaf or a blackguard. As much as he could, he rolled to his side, freeing the soft creature. His back leaned against hard, rounded sticks. Legs of the sofa? Maybe they weren't in a grave. Well, not yet.

"Speak to me. Are you well?" Her voice was sweet and filled with a level of calm he wouldn't expect in a woman or anyone else in this situation.

His pride dropped to his gut. He'd been weak and unconscious, lying atop her. With as much poise as he could muster, he said, "My head throbs, and my back has seen better days. How 'bout you?"

"You weren't moving. I thought you were dying." Her voice was low but filled with genuine concern. His time in Rundle's circles showed him the difference.

He flattened their linked palms against his waistcoat. Together, they'd feel the rapid punches of his heart. "See. Still here. Are you injured?"

Her legs shifted against his. "I can move. My shins were quite pinned."

She was kind, not pointing out the obvious. His heavy leg had held her limbs in place. Every muscle attached to his spine stung, but knowing she'd survived without injury lessened the pain. A strong soul coursed inside this woman. Nothing hysterical or fragile about her. Something a man should fight for, hope to possess.

"You could hemorrhage. I read in a book—"

"Shhh. Be careful of what you read." He hoped his voice sounded light and humorous. "What's another bruise, my lady?"

The sound of her chuckles was better than Christmas bells. Without a doubt, he'd let the world fall upon him again if it meant being this close to an angel. "Though this was a library, not much reading will be done here today, Lady Charm….Duchess."

"Call me Charlotte. Might as well if these are our last moments."

Surely, God wouldn't let him be this

close to an angel only to witness her death. He released her and started moving his hands along the floor. "I'm not ready for my final hours."

His thumb traced the grains of the boards. If he could find a worn patch, he might be able to wedge them out and slip her through. Unlike him, she was thin enough to drop between the support joists and into the cellar. Flattening his hand, he searched anew.

She stiffened and pushed away from his flailing arms. "What are you doing?"

"I'm looking for a seam."

She slapped his face. "You'll not be finding one of mine, even if we are going to die."

His head throbbed as he blocked her next thrust with his forearm. He gripped her hand and pressed her slim fingers against the flooring. "You have nothing—I repeat, nothing—to worry about. I may be of the merchant class, but I know my place. It's not to seek an advantage."

A sigh binding up his frustrations leapt from his nostrils. He lowered his tone, bottling up the sting of her words. She must not think well of him. "My sister might be lost, stranded with a stranger, and I'd hope the fellow, gentleman or not, would look to keep her safe rather than attempting a compromise."

She tightened her hand about his. "I'm sorry."

In the jet-black air, he couldn't see her, but he could feel her moving closer to him. A small whiff of lavender touched his nose before it clogged with dust. "If we find a loose board, I might be able to pry it up and get you to the cellar before this space falls in."

A gentle palm met his jaw, caressing where she'd just struck. "Just me?"

He probably wouldn't fit between the floor joists. It didn't matter. No sounds of rescue arose above the harsh wind. Everyone was too busy aiding the other guests—that is, if any survived. "Let's work together."

Pushing, fingering for a crevice, he forced his mind away from thoughts that Lillian, Lord Rundle, or even Theol, had perished with the house. God must not let that happen.

With a shake of his head, he focused on what he could do to save the duchess. After poking and smoothing, he found a split as wide as his index finger among loose floorboards. Hallelujah. He might be able to save this fiery angel.

Charlotte stared into the dark space, failing miserably to ignore the creaking and shifting of their makeshift ceiling or the smell of pitch, which oozed from everywhere. If Mr. Cinder were correct, how much time did they have before this pocket collapsed?

Her pulse raced. She hadn't lived enough to die now.

"Duchess, are you sure you're not injured? You're shaking my elbow." His velvet voice wrapped about her, bolstering her resolve.

She willed away the trembles. "I'm just cold, and I asked you to call me Charlotte."

"Yes, ma'am, Duchess."

Were those chuckles in his response? " Difficult man. You don't accept instruction well."

"Depends." His finger slipped under her side, moving against her ribs, almost tickling. He pulled his hands away. "Please Lord, I got one board free. Help me get another."

Maybe only men could hear Providence's words. She waited, hoping to hear words of confirmation. A minute passed and she heard nothing. "Ask Him again."

"What?" Mr. Cinder shifted his leg away from hers. "One of my shoes is gone. It's blown clean off."

What kind of confirmation was that? Before she could inquire, the earth above shuddered and rained dirt and leaves of paper. Charlotte balled her fists and beat upon the floor. "It's not fair. No one should be hurt because of some wind."

He claimed both her hands and towed them to his chest. "Don't lose your clear head, not now."

Her fingers sank against the hard sinews, the strength burning within his silken waist-coat. The world creaked above their heads, showering dust. Closing her eyes, she pushed closer to the silk until she felt his arms surrounding her.

The tremors stopped, but her hero held her.

"Everything will be fine. I'll get you out of here for your coronation."

"A presentation, funny man." His attempt at humor didn't settle the anxiety swirling within her bosom.

"Aren't you ladies presented all the time? Lord knows Ella's has sold a great deal for come-outs and the theater, and—"

"My first one. My mother died right before I was to be presented. Then Papa and I were too busy traveling to have a season."

A creak and pop above couldn't drown the satisfaction in his tone. "I'd miss a season to travel. From what I hear, the endless fretting of beaus and baubles is too much. Well, it keeps my Ella's in business."

Her eyes stung. Tears wetted her lashes. "Why do you joke? It is important. A man—even one who makes heavenly crea-tions—wouldn't understand. You fellows get world tours and college."

"Not all of us." He sighed long and hard.

"I've never traveled or ventured out of London. I have fabrics imported from Italy. A crate has seen more than me."

She knew that feeling of longing, of hoping the world would slow down so she could catch up. Shaking, she pushed aside yesterday's regrets and focused on now, the comfort of having someone else with her in this nightmare. "When the room collapsed, you weren't moving. I don't want to be alone."

He stroked her arms, the curve of her shoulders. "I'm not finished yet. Keep talking. I love your voice. It helps you think, right?"

His teasing was gentle, his touch reassuring, but Charlotte was not to be comforted. Her final moments should be honest ones. "You took the brunt of the ceiling, just like the sign. I didn't thank you in Cheapside. I don't even know your whole name."

His soft breath, smelling of honey, grazed her forehead. "It's Edwin, Edwin Cinder."

The floor groaned. The world shook. The weight of everything would soon come down and suffocate them, but she enjoyed snuggling within his arms. "Thank you for protecting me, Edwin Cinder."

With a final squeeze, he pivoted, slipping her against the hard legs of the sofa. His arms fell away as he moved to the edge of their cocoon. "Don't give up yet. This floor's shifting.

We can get you to the cellar."

Again, he talked of saving her. What manner of man was this? Never had she met anyone so self-sacrificing.

"Duchess, search the floor. I had a spoon on me. It's not in my pocket. If I had it, I could make quicker work of prying free this plank."

In the darkness, she couldn't make out what he did, but absorbed the vibration of his taps along the boards. A breeze flew from his swinging arms.

Charlotte tugged off her gloves and smoothed the floor beneath her. A couple inches under the skirting of the sofa, she caught a cold metal implement. It had to be his spoon. "Here."

He took it, his warm fingers touching her bare ones. "That should do it."

Pop. Click. "I have another board free. Not much longer, Duchess."

With a grunt and a groan, Edwin wiggled more boards loose and laid them gently by her fingers. "I've got the hole big enough. I'll lower you through. Ready?"

She pulled herself to the hole. It wasn't dark below. A lit bit of light shone. "Yes. I think I can make it."

He took her hand within his large palm. "You'll be in the cellar. The halls should be lit because of the wine stock for the party."

Holding her breath, she stuck her feet into the hole and slid between the tight boards. Dangling, she strengthened her grip on his forearm.

"You will be fine." His voice sounded strong and calm. "The cellar is shallow. Let go."

Looking up into the dark room, she couldn't see Edwin's face, so she let go. Her feet almost instantly hit the ground. She was free. "Your turn."

"Grab a candle and work your way past the coal room. There should be a servants' door to lead you to the mews or the street."

He didn't even try to fit through. Frustrated, her fists balled. "You have to try."

"No, Duchess, I don't. I can't fit. Go on. There's not much time before it all falls in."

Her heart lurched as she turned from him and started toward the light. How could she think of abandoning him, the bravest, most self-sacrificing man in the world? No, she couldn't. She pivoted toward the hole. "I'm not moving."

"You must. Don't let me die in vain. Please go, angel." His voice slowed as if he struggled for air. "For pity's sake, go."

She didn't know what was worse. Leaving her hero to die beneath the debris of the crumbling library or being told what to do.

Edwin lay against the floor as his makeshift prison shifted, the ceiling lowering. The sofa puffed and whined. It wouldn't support the mass much longer. It would be over soon. At least the duchess, Charlotte, would survive. Hopefully, she'd retell his story with kindness, how the hapless tradesman saved her. Maybe she'd be charitable at the next ball to another misfit.

But the thought of her dancing in another's arms made his inwards knot. Could he be smitten so soon, so quickly?

The thought of finding love at last should lessen the pain of dying. Funny. Moments ago, he felt alone in a library. Now he was alone, buried in rubble, but his heart felt full.

"Lord, let Charlotte and Lillian live and have good lives."

With a deep breath, he folded his arms behind his head. He closed his eyes and tried to remember how nice it felt to comfort Charlotte, the slim weight of her nestled in his arms. Yes, that was a dream to have stuck in his head as death visited.

Whack!

The ground beneath him shook. The tremors of Fairwilde wouldn't quit.

Wham! This time a chunk of wood flew up from the hole, missing his nose by an inch.

He heard Charlotte wheeze, but her voice

sounded strong, determined. "Edwin, just a few more hits with this ax and the hole will be large enough for you to slip through."

He edged closer to the opening and waved his arms to keep from being accidentally impaled. "You need to give up. Breaking the floor joists will weaken the whole structure. The cellar could fall in much faster."

"It's a risk we'll both have to take. Now sit back." She hefted the ax above her shoulder. The lit torch upon the wall made her look fierce, with yards of golden curls falling down her back. Her long neck craned toward him; those haunting blue eyes pierced his soul. "Edwin, move before debris hits you."

He did as she commanded, but a new fear entered his skull. What if she did free him, and somehow they survived? Could he forget this feeling of love building within his chest?

Beads of perspiration formed on Charlotte's brow. She brushed them away, then hefted the ax once more. Her first couple of haphazard strokes made a deep cut in the crossbeam, but she needed to cut through this second section for the obstruction to fall away and free Edwin.

Her heart beat so hard her ears hurt. She lowered the ax to the dirt floor and rested upon it. "Edwin, are you still there?"

"Yes."

The monotone voice yielded no encouragement. He must expect her to give up and leave him in the debris. She couldn't do that, not to the man who'd saved her life twice. "I'm going to liberate you, but talk to me. Maybe tell me about how you make such exquisite shoes. No, better tell how you will give me the fairy slippers in the glass case when I free you."

No answer. She'd have to prove it to him. Sucking in a breath, she raised the ax and struck the ceiling beam. Dust and bits of wood fell. She blinked heavily, clearing her eyes. This rescue business was taxing.

And so was swinging the ax. How did Papa's grooms make it look so easy?

She peered up at the hole in the ceiling. "Edwin, if you're not going to hold up your side of this conversation… My, how pigheaded you are. You should give me the special pair and something else." She wiped more sweat on her dirty, shredded sleeve. "And it should be lilac. I'll be getting a new dress after tonight, for this frock will be retired."

With a grunt, she hefted the ax. Wham. Another inch or two and she'd cut through. "Edwin, is it a deal?"

"Stop. Leave me. You're going to hurt yourself." There was an edge in his voice as if he was exasperated.

How could he be tired? He wasn't the one swinging the ax. "Men. Can't stand for a woman to exert power."

"Duchess, you don't seem willing to listen."

She took another heavy hit, then lowered the tool. Leaning against the long handle, she filled her lungs. The sweet, cold air of the cellar took away the heat filling her insides. "You mean I don't do as I am told. I've set my mind on freeing you. That is what I'm going to do."

"Please, exit the cellar. At least you'd be safe from Fairwilde's shakings. Maybe you could find someone to help. I know you're tired."

She slurped in the scream wanting to leap from her lips as her blade whacked the beam. The ache in her arms increased as she swung again. "You mean find some *man* to help."

No, she was doing what she wanted. Right now, nothing was more important than saving Edwin.

"Dearest Charlotte, it's not a defeat to seek help." His voice tapered to a whisper.

Dearest? The endearment sounded right coming from Edwin. She shook her head. Sentiment couldn't distract her. "If that is so, why do you want me to stop?"

This time she didn't wait for him to respond. With a grunt, she powered the blade with everything in her. She hit the beam and the ax sliced through. The obstinate section fell. The wooden chunk dropped into the dirt and bounced very close to her slippers. Something stung her ankle, but all she could do was look up and marvel at the gap she'd made. Without that piece of wood narrowing the hole, Edwin should be able to slip through. "I've done it! Give it a try."

His head appeared above the hole. With pursed lips, his fingers traced the span. "You may have."

His thick mop disappeared, but one stocking-clad foot and one with a slipper took its place. Soon all of him—long legs, wide chest, and endless arms—dropped inside.

Edwin now towered above her again.

She let the ax fall from her fingers. Her gaze locked with his as a smile lifted his lips. The urge to wrap her tired arms about his neck nearly overwhelmed her sense of etiquette.

He took a step toward her as a crashing noise sounded overhead.

A timber the length of a tree trunk fell through the hole and crashed to the floor, kicking up a thick cloud of dust. The torch she'd stuck on the wall flickered and almost extinguished. She shut her lids tight.

The hole from which Edwin had just dropped closed completely. Another minute, and Edwin would've been crushed under the weight of that beam. Her sore arms started to shake.

Yet as the creaking above started to subside, warmth swaddled her. Her shoulders slumped, and she leaned into the welcoming embrace.

Opening her eyes, she found Edwin holding her. His chin rested atop her head. His gentle words, maybe a verse or a whispered prayer, caressed her ears. Even if the world fell down upon them, she'd never feel safer, or more like she belonged.

Such a silly notion. She gripped his lapels and drew closer to him. A tremble started in her fingers and rippled down to her toes.

"You're shivering." Edwin released her, stripped off his tailcoat, and spread it upon her shoulders. "That should keep you."

It wasn't the cold air making her shake. It was the beating of his heart against her ear. And the sudden answer of hers as it met the rhythm.

That was downright frightening. Illogical. He was a stranger.

Probably the most handsome stranger she'd ever met. She clutched the silver buttons of his jacket and kept herself from running back into his arms.

"Cold cellar." He leaned against the threshold. "The ingress is one of the strongest parts of a room. We should be safe, for the moment."

She squinted at him. The low light of the

torch made his eyes seem big, like a squirrel's. One gnawing a hidden nut. "You knew."

He tugged at his wilted cravat. "Knew what?"

"You knew our pocket was going to fall in and didn't think I could get you out."

"I'd rather you were safe than fussing about me." His gaze broke from hers and lowered. "The ribbon on your shoe is sheared. It has splinters. Let me—"

She put a hand on his shoulder, stopping him from descending. Shoes, though she loved them, didn't matter. "You truly were ready to die."

A blast of air released from his nose. He stood erect. "I didn't want to, but I'm not afraid. I'm secure in my salvation."

"You are so young. Still probably in your twenties, with plenty of life to live. How can you be so? Does God talk to you and guide you?"

"I just know. I put my trust in Him and now a duchess. A wonderful duchess." Edwin's voice tapered off as his head swiveled to the dark hall. "You'll make some lucky gentleman very proud." He cleared his throat. "Let's see about getting out of here."

What? How could he pay her such a compliment, then move away? Wasn't she pretty enough for him? Maybe too demanding, too assertive like Papa.

He eased back into the room and grabbed the torch and the ax she'd dropped. With careful steps, he returned to her and craned his head to the left, in the direction of the coal room, where she'd found the blessed blade. "This way to freedom."

The moment of softness—of vulnerability—fled, hiding within Edwin's steeled tone. It had to be for the best. A few more minutes of knowing a strong man like Papa trusted her, and it would be her undoing. All reason would leave and she'd confess feelings her heart couldn't possibly possess, not after knowing Edwin for only an evening.

CHAPTER FIVE

The Cellar

dwin trudged down the corridor. His steps were slow, and it wasn't because one foot was shoe-less. His heart was cleaved.

Never, ever had he been jealous of his step-brother or any of the gentlefolk customers who patronized his shops. Now he understood the truth of Theol's insult, about Edwin being a man of low birth. What right did Edwin have to love a duchess or to expect her love in return?

The God he loved with all his soul had just knocked down Fairwilde. Now He filled Edwin's heart with admiration for a brave, unattainable woman. A grunt left his lips. Ridiculous. Maybe he had more dreamer in his blood than he suspected.

"Are you injured?" Charlotte's soft palm clutched his forearm. Her chilled digits sliced through the thin silk of his shirt, icing each hurting tendon and muscle. A taste for more set upon his tongue. Bitter dregs followed when she pulled away.

He shook his foolish head. "Beyond the coal room is the door to the mews. That is our path to freedom."

"But that way is blocked. Part of the house has come down there. It's still rumbling. "

"No. That's under the dining room." He charged forward. "My family." Woolen knit slipping, his one slipper slapping at the tiled path, he slid around the corner.

A high mound of broken beams and furnishings piled from the floor to the remnants of the ceiling.

All the air fled his lungs.

A torn tablecloth, formerly bleached snow white, flopped like a broken coat of arms. Sparkling bits of glass and silvery crushed objects, symbols of Fairwilde's glory, lay trashed at his feet.

One pant followed another as he relearned to breathe. "Why, Lord?"

Impenetrable, massive, wholly destroyed. All of Mama and Lord Rundle's precious home, knocked to rubble. This was so far from the glittering palace-like place he'd first seen at sixteen.

Charlotte's hand again draped his shoulder.

"I am so sorry, Edwin."

He seized it, linking his fingers with hers and tugging the union close to his heart. She was real, an anchor in the windstorm.

"Edwin, say something. Let me help." She drew him into a hug and held him tight.

When he found his voice, it was low and garbled. "Mother loved this house." He coughed up the dust thick in the air. "She and Lord Rundle, they'd only been married a year when she had the chandelier restrung and gave a party to celebrate her sending me off to a year of tutors."

"The chandelier was beautiful tonight as we danced." Her hold didn't lessen, and he didn't want it to disappear. "My father provided nothing but the best tutors for me. It was good of Rundle and your mother to do that."

"It was terrifying. The stores were run by middle managers. My mother was overworked, all so I could go from figurin' to calculations." He pointed to shards of crystal anointing the floor. "Now her labors are broken glass."

"It can be rebuilt, the fixtures remade."

"Perhaps." A glint, a shimmer caught his gaze. He bolted from Charlotte and tugged at the fabric until he'd freed it. In his palm lay a silvery glove with shiny glass beads trimming the hem. His sister's glove.

Heart splitting open, he crumpled to his knees. "God! She can't be dead."

The water building in his eyes almost broke free. He bit his lip. Losing more of his composure in front of Charlotte simply could not be done.

"What a pretty glove. Edwin. That young girl who happened upon us after we danced... Edwin?"

How could he respond to the sweet voice and not release the battle stewing within his bones? Droplets leaked down his face. *My poor Lillian.* She hadn't lived yet.

Charlotte stooped in front of him. Her dainty pinkie swiped from the corner of his eye to the bridge of his nose. "That was your sister, wasn't she? It doesn't mean she's gone. We must think well."

He focused not on the wonderful angel whose simple act of kindness could melt his bones, but the mound that stole his sister. Hands shaking, he leapt up and pulled at a beam. Nothing would keep him from Lillian.

The earth shook and more debris fell. Charlotte folded her arms and tried to figure out how to calm Edwin. He wasn't acting rational. How could she stop the enraged man from bringing down the rest of the roof?

The dainty glove lay at her feet. She scooped it up, then hopped backward out of the range of flying debris. "Edwin, you have to stop."

"My sister." His voice was raw and dry. "That is her glove. She must be under that pile."

"You don't know that. It might be one that looks similar."

"I know fabric, cut, and style." He strained and pulled at a joist, a heavy eight-inch section of broken beam. "It's hers."

Think, Charlotte. Save him from himself. "She's not under this pile. A proper young lady removes her gloves before dinner." She looked down at her own naked, dirty palms. "Or when she's looking for a spoon or wielding an ax. All other times, she'd wear gloves."

She took a few steps and crossed in front of him. "Your sister probably sat down, readying for dinner, then ran out like the rest of Fairwilde when the damage occurred."

He blinked and lowered his arms to his sides. Her logic must be reaching him.

Easing closer, near enough to see the golden flecks in his watery eyes, she took hold of his hands. "If you were my brother, I'd want you safe above ground and with other men who can lift and help with all this rubble. And maybe your sister is outside, hoping for some sign of you. Don't you think we should get out of here and go find her?"

His brow crinkled, and he looked down at his wiggling toes. "How can you be so confident?"

"I know the turmoil you are feeling. The helplessness. I watched my father run himself ragged. He wouldn't listen until he expired. If he'd heeded, we might have had more time." She swallowed the self-pity bubbling within her throat and focused on the pain radiating from Edwin's slumping posture. "I just know, inside, your sister is well. My companion is well, too. We both have to trust."

He wrenched at the back of his neck. His broad shoulders squared as if he were called to attention. "You asked if God speaks to me. It's not always words, but it's a confident feeling that all will be well. It burns my gut, makes my steps clearer. I trust you are hearing truth. I trust you."

The look in his eyes, penetrating, soul-stirring, burned almost as much as his answer. She'd been seeking direction. Maybe God had implanted his answers inside all along. She latched onto his arm. "We need to get out of here. Is there another way?"

"The coal chute. We might be able to get out that way, but it will be very dirty."

She held up her arms, displaying the stains on her striped gown, then pushed at her deflated cap sleeves. "I can't get much worse. We need to go find our love ones."

His head nodded, but his gaze shifted toward the debris. "What if you are wrong? And I gave up before I could help her?"

"If she's under this pile, you can't help her. That debris weighs tons. We need to get more people to dig through this." She tucked her palm on his elbow and turned him in the opposite direction. "If I am wrong, I'll stand with you and help you with the grief. I'm an expert. Hurting yourself by causing a cave-in will do no good."

Her insides warmed. She could feel with confidence that all would be well. "When I am right, you will give me the fairy slippers. Shall we wager?"

He shook his head but clasped her palm. "Let's head back to the fuel room and see if we can make it out through the coal chute."

Arm in arm they trudged down the hall. His deep voice echoed. "You're not getting those shoes, but I'll make you something personally for your royal presentation. I have to reward you somehow."

"I want what I want—the ones I saw in your shop. Nothing else could be as fine."

He spun her into the coal room. "If I make them for you, it will be. Trust in me as I do you."

Part of her wanted to turn from his gaze. It was too warm, and hers probably reflected frightening emotions of commitment and love.

"I suppose a two-heart minimum is still required for those precious slippers."

Reaching toward her ear, he smoothed a wild tendril from her cheek. "Let's climb out of here and find my sister and the other survivors."

The feel of his rough palm sent shivers down her spine. If he'd leaned down and kissed her, she wouldn't have stopped him. The need to know what it would be like to have his lips upon hers made logic leach from her pores. She wiped her damp hands on her tattered bodice, her fingers smoothing the smudged ruffles.

He hooked her pinkie with his. His gaze bored down on her. "I've never seen a more beautiful woman. Don't fret."

She couldn't look away or imagine how he could view her as such. Her dress was filthy. Who knows how horrid her falling curls looked.

Yet he didn't move, didn't turn his head.

Her pulse ramped as she put a hand to his jaw. She was ready to give the down payment for the slippers: her heart.

The look in Charlotte's eyes—soft, wanting, searching—forced Edwin to garner an uneasy breath. She couldn't know how the light in her eyes heated his soul, made him wish for things he could never claim...like possessing her love, marrying her.

With a shake of his head, he stepped backward and yanking off his deflated cravat. "The chute. If it's not blocked at the street, we could climb out."

He grasped the biggest log he could find from a pile of neatly stacked wood, then hefted it into the rectangular groove cut in the wall. Thrusting with all his might, he hit and twisted his weapon up the chute.

Coal ash filled the air. Choking, he lowered the heavy log and spun toward Charlotte. "I think I'll see moonlight soon, but this is horrid work."

"You're doing what has to be done. You're not a passive man, Edwin Cinder." She stood at his side, fanning her dainty button nose. The light of the wall torch made her eyes sparkle. So pretty and independent.

His attraction didn't matter. He had to protect her with everything in him, including keeping her safe from his own desires. He picked up the log again and heaved, one powerful hit for every reason a duchess and a shoe peddler couldn't be together.

Whack! Crack. The obstruction gave way. Moonlight crept inside.

"You did it. It looks wide enough." With a palm on his shoulder, she stood on tiptoes and angled her long neck toward their stone pathway to the surface.

The lavender fragrance in her hair had dissipated, replaced with hints of pitch and wood dust, but the desire to sink his fingers into her locks and weave it about his hand remained. The pull to tow her into his arms pressed at his lungs, draining away his will to resist.

"Now." His voice cracked, and he coughed. "Now's not the time to dawdle. Freedom will be ours with a few more hits with this log."

Pivoting, she planted herself in front of him and did not move her hand from his sleeve. Her bright eyes locked with his as moon rays encircled them. "Only a few more moments, and we'll find out how everyone faired. I meant what I said about standing by you."

In spite of their circumstances, their differences in rank and a ton of rubble over their heads, did she know how kissable she seemed? Did she want his caress? Maybe she did.

He set down the log. "Duchess, I've never been good at the art of flirting. What is it you want of me?"

Her cheeks darkened almost to the shading of the coal ash tingeing her countenance. "May I reward my hero with a proper kiss?"

It was wrong. He shouldn't, but his head dipped anyway. He slid his arms about her and held her close. His lips brushed hers, and she did not pull away.

Instead, her palms swept about his neck as

she sought his mouth. Fire burnt his skin as she allowed a deeper kiss. He completely forgot about his duty to protect her reputation and even shield his heart as she strengthened her hold, and he surrendered to the love boiling in his veins. She scorched his tongue with an inferno of sweetness. This feeling of heaven mixed with a loss of control wouldn't be extinguished. The silk of her skin, the lulling moan as she murmured his name, branded his chest.

"Hallo! Any one down there?" The interruption bellowed down the shaft.

He leapt from her and hid her behind his back. "Yes, Cinder and the Duchess of Charming are down here. Can you remove the debris and help me get her to safety?"

"Yes, Mr. Cinder. I'll be back with more men." The voices fell away but for distant shouts of, "Over here. Help!"

He pivoted and glanced at the most beautiful woman in all of England, the one he still wanted in his arms. But kissing a lady not pledged to him was wrong. "We'll be free in a few minutes, Duchess."

She nodded and put a hand to her reddened lips. Her eyes did not lift again. She must be filled with regret.

His one moment of dreaming had gone awry. He blinked hard, then focused on the ground. "Don't worry. I'll protect your reputation. I won't kiss and tell, or compromise you. We can pretend this never happened. If all our loved ones are well, we can forget this night."

"If that's what you want, Mr. Cinder." She put her back to him and marched to the opening.

Was that hurt in her voice?

Before he could answer, shouts came closer. More light poured through the shaft. The rescuers must've pried open the chute.

"We can lift you out. It's a tight fit, but we've got you. Let's get the duchess out first." Hands stretched down.

She looked over her shoulder as she clutched the dangling arms and began her ascent to the surface. Tears filled her gentle eyes before she disappeared.

His heart shrank in response.

Minutes ago, he could only think of his family and how their loss would end his world. Now, his head filled with regret. How would he get on with Charlotte slipping away from him?

CHAPTER SIX

Before Midnight

Charlotte waited in her carriage, huddled in the damp blanket a rescuer had given her. Her hands fidgeted, and she turned to the window to gaze at the coal chute. It had been a nasty fit, but the men had pulled her through it. Edwin was larger with the broadest shoulders. How would he escape the cellar?

A distant chime of a church bell announced the half hour. Soon it would be midnight. How long would poor Edwin languish, not knowing freedom—a few more minutes, or another hour?

Her stomach clenched and she pressed against her torn bodice. Scratchy concrete had brushed against her and painted her in soot. The soft glow of the carriage lantern exposed her ripped lilac skirt. Filthy, dressed in rags, would Edwin still think her beautiful?

A shudder raced through her tired limbs. What if Edwin were stuck? What if the roof in the coal room fell on top of him? The lone beating of her heart answered her meandering thoughts. A part of her cared too much for this virtual stranger with autumn-kissed eyes. Yes, something deep inside wanted his arms about her, covering her in safety.

Willing away the urge to run back to the coal chute, she pushed at her hair, trying to restore her chignon. With no pins left to speak of, she gave up and let the tangled gold fall back to her limp shoulders.

If she ordered her thoughts, then maybe she could regain her senses and know with certainty that love didn't stir in her bosom. Only foolish women could claim to have found love after a few hours. She snatched her arms tight about her. Charlotte, the Duchess of Charming, was not foolish.

"Over here!" The shout bellowed in the dark.

She stretched and leaned closer to the carriage glass.

Dozens came running, hefting and yanking at debris. Lanterns swung, shedding light over a pile of broken beams and scattered bricks tossed about the lawn. The endless destruction looked as if a great giant had picked up the home, crumpled its wall, and tossed it from the clouds.

A sigh wrapped in sorrow oozed from her throat. Fairwilde was gone. *Lord God, let Edwin's family have survived.*

The door opened letting in chilly air. Lord Cheshire had escorted Mercy back to the carriage. Good old Mercy, alive and well; the first person to embrace her upon exiting Fairwilde. Charlotte swiped at fresh tears as her friend with the duke's assistance climbed inside. "Thank you, Duke."

He nodded. The tall man cast weary eyes upon her. "Are you well, Duchess?"

No, she wasn't, but who would be after a night like this? "I'm not injured, but please see about Mr. Cinder. They haven't freed him from the cellar."

"I will." He nodded. "Cinder's a good man." The tails of the duke's jacket bore tears and dust. The man had born the gale's fury, probably crawling through debris to save people.

Maybe she could ask about Edwin's family without giving away her heart's pain. She schooled her face and tried a light voice. "Sir, did Lord Rundle and his daughter...?" She swallowed the fear ramping inside. "And his other son, are they alive?"

The duke rubbed his forehead as his gaze lowered to the floor. "Lord Rundle isn't doing well. He took the brunt of the falling chandelier, but Miss Rundle and Lord Theol are not injured."

An easier breath filled Charlotte's lungs. At least Edwin's sister was well, but how would he take the news of his stepfather?

The duke tapped along the doorframe as if to end her woolgathering, but how could she not be distracted?

"Duchess, tomorrow, I will come see you. There is something your father and I discussed before he passed. I must seek your opinion on the matter." He bowed and closed the door.

Mercy put her hands to her chubby face. "The widowed duke is going to make you an offer. Oh my."

"Don't be ridiculous. Cheshire was an associate of my father. He's more like an uncle than a beau."

"He's not that old. He's respectable, rich, and a gentleman." Mercy tugged at the netting cowl of her gown, attempting to secure her jiggling womanhood. "Everything your father would want."

Charlotte couldn't think of others' expectations. Only Edwin and his safety filled her head. She covered her face. "Stop, Mercy. No more pushing, not tonight."

Her friend caught Charlotte's fingers, pulling them to the seat. "I do so, for your future, duchess. It's what your father wanted."

"It's not about my father's will. I want to choose. I know my mind."

The edge in her voice evaporated her companion's cheer. The woman's head lowered. "I just want you to be happy. I know I push, even sending you out in this evil storm, but I mean nothing but good."

Charlotte's heart softened toward her busybody friend. She tugged the blanket closer. For a few seconds she imagined the encompassing wool was Edwin warming her. Was he frightened? Did he miss her? No, he said to forget everything. She blinked her eyes and directed her gaze back to her downcast friend. "You are the dearest of women, even with your pushing. I would never have survived this past year without you."

Mercy's round face rose. "You are shaking." She splayed her fingers along Charlotte's brow. "You don't have a fever."

"No, Mercy. I'm well." She tried to force her teeth into a sunny umbrella smile, but the frown swallowing her companion's countenance indicated an utter failure.

Bonnet-less and coat-less, Mercy fidgeted and took a handkerchief from her pocket. Bare hands. Had she left her gloves at the dinner table, too?

"I had the footman warm the space. I knew

if you lived..." The poor woman's eyes grew large, like a frog who'd swallowed its tongue.

Charlotte glanced again at the group of men gathered around the coal chute. No Edwin yet. She shivered and pivoted to her friend. "I survived. Think no more of this."

"How can I not? I made you come." Mercy clasped her elbows as if the woman's limbs would fall off. "What a wasted evening. Yet, if the duke makes an offer... Oh, let me stop running on. I can at least get you home before midnight. That is what I promised."

"No." The word exited Charlotte's mouth too strongly.

Mercy looked aghast with her mouth hanging open, lips dangling. "I thought you wanted to leave before midnight."

Steam piped out of Charlotte's nose. She let her legs sink into the cushions of the seat. Part of her heart was very glad to attend, glad of every moment she'd spent with Edwin. Pity he wanted to forget everything. "I'm sorry. I don't mean to be cross, but we are not leaving, not until Mr. Cinder is safe from the crumbling Fairwilde."

"I see." Her companion opened a jar of mustard-smelling liniment. "The doctors have been running about helping folks. He put this on my wrist. Surely, it will make all your bruises feel better. If we must sit here, put it on to get relief."

It would need to be applied everywhere, but only after a simmering bath. Charlotte shook her head, then twisted again to see out of the glass. "Why is it taking so long to free one man?"

There was no way she could leave without knowing Edwin was safe. He might pretend nothing happened, but he was still the man who'd saved her life. The man she knew she cared for like no other.

Her ash-stained hands fisted. How could he pretend nothing happened? Forget her toes curling when he kissed her or the strength of his arms about her waist? Her heart surely burst when he whispered *sweetest girl* low in her ear. Men must be made of stone, so different from her.

Mercy fidgeted as the wind rattled the carriage glass. "The wind is coming again."

"The worst has to be over. There's nothing left here to be knocked down." She snuggled into Edwin's jacket underneath the wool blanket, but her trembles returned. With a grunt, she willed her limbs to stop and rotated to the window. Was the death toll high? Not everyone had an Edwin Cinder to protect them. "The duke said Lord Rundle was injured. Did you see the earl?"

"Yes, Lord Cheshire and the daughter had

to pull the fellow from the ruins. The old man was barely conscious. His head bled."

"Oh no. Maybe a surgeon could fix him." A long breath poured out from Charlotte's sinking heart. "At least Edwin's sister is safe."

"Edwin, is it now?"

Cheeks warming, she avoided the smirk filling Mercy's countenance and sat back, fingering the buttons on his jacket. "He will be relieved that his sister is well. Hopefully he can get to Lord Rundle before... Oh, let's pray everything will be well."

Charlotte meant her promise to stand by him through his loss, as much as she had the kiss, but he wouldn't let her. She stopped squeezing his buttons, before one popped off. "We'll have the footman clean Mr. Cinder's cloak and return it—I guess to Ella's—tomorrow. It should still be standing."

"Lord Cheshire said chimneys and buildings have fallen all over London." Mercy reached over with a handkerchief and scrubbed at Charlotte's chin. "You need a bath. Several baths. Oh, let's get the carriage going and not waste another minute at foul Fairwilde."

"I have to know that Edwin is safe."

Mercy lifted her hand and pointed to the window. "There's your *Edwin* now."

Blinking, Charlotte's gaze heated with the sight of him. Tall, handsome, he leaned on the shoulders of the duke of Cheshire and Lord Rundle's giant butler. As Edwin's gaze turned her direction, her breath caught. Was he hurt?

Her feelings for him were so strong and true, they stung her bosom. How could he not want her?

Mercy lifted her chin. "Maybe we should invite him inside?"

What would she say to Edwin? *Please love me?* Never. "Let's go before the bells' final chime. He's safe. We'll send servants back to help with the injured. The more men to help the better." She tapped the roof. At Grosvenor Square, she'd drown her sorrows in a bath of steamy lavender. She smelled the musty perspiration in her sleeves. A thousand tubs of water would do.

Lord Cheshire and Abraham lowered Edwin to the ground. The squeeze of the tight chute took all his breath.

"Let's give him a moment." The duke stepped back, his head turning to the line of carriages.

Abraham shook his head and hovered. "Not leaving you, sir. Rundle's orders."

The man's large shadow didn't block the rain. The small drizzle felt good atop Edwin's brow. The fishy stench of whale-blubber torches surrounded him. The flames added an orange tinge to the moonlit air. He could see the broken chute in which he'd become wedged, the rescuers' chisels, and piles of scattered bricks and demolished furniture. A gulp of air stuck in his throat. Fairwilde was gone.

With a shake of his head, he pushed up from the sidewalk. Standing upright with no sign or beam overhead to drop upon him, he gulped some of the cool breeze. It had been foolish to try to scramble after Charlotte through such a tight space. Stupid coal chute. Stupid Edwin.

The bruising along his ribs prevented a full breath from reaching his lungs. Head feeling light, he started to keel over.

"Hold on, Cinder." Cheshire caught him before he hit the sidewalk. "Easy."

Edwin hooked one arm around the duke and the other around Lord Rundle's stalwart Abraham. "Sorry, I didn't think I was so unsteady."

The duke eased him back to the ground. "'Twas a fool's notion to try to squeeze out of that chute. You're a large fellow. I suppose you were anxious to get out of Fairwilde. Maybe put your head between your legs to restore the blood flow."

It wasn't anxiety. It was fear, fear he'd given up something wonderful, life-changing. He should've confessed his true feelings to Charlotte while he had the chance. Being noble to protect her reputation seemed right, but maybe it was a coward's doing.

"Where is your shoe? You've one missing." Abraham looked from side to side. His jaw clenched as if he were in pain. "There's so much broken glass you might hurt yourself."

Edwin waved his arms to stop the fussing. "Please just tell me, now that I've been chiseled out of the chute, is...are Lillian and my stepfather alive? Theol?"

Abraham's full lips pressed together as an audible swallow vibrated in his throat. His shoulders sagged beneath his dusty livery. "Yes, Mr. Cinder. And your stepbrother, too. But Lord Rundle was hurt bad in the falling of the house. The doctors were with him before he sent me back here for you. I put them in your residence in Cheapside."

Edwin rubbed his brow as his heart clenched. Poor Rundle. "Did Theol make a fuss squatting in the mercantile part of London?"

Abraham's lean cheek trembled. "He drowned his mighty sorrows in liquor."

A dark carriage etched with a gleaming coat of armor scattered moon rays as it flew past. The wheels splashed water from the myriad of puddles lining the street.

Charlotte. He didn't have to see her face to know for sure, but his pulse slowed as if she'd left his life again.

"The duchess was particularly concerned about you, Cinder." Cheshire drew his arms behind his back. "The lady seemed well, after this harrowing ordeal."

The chime of a church bell moaned, the final toll of midnight. This awful day was done. Edwin closed his eyes for a moment and relived holding Charlotte by the couch, in the threshold after she rescued him. The look in her eyes before they kissed stamped his brain. "She's the bravest, sweetest lass I know."

"Cinder?" The duke's forehead furrowed. "What happened down in the cellar?"

What could Edwin say that wouldn't hurt Charlotte's reputation? His brain wasn't working well enough to forestall an interrogation. Once he checked on Lord Rundle and Lillian, he could take a moment to puzzle things out, maybe even venture to see Charlotte. Lord Rundle would know where she lived. Edwin pulled to his feet, then offered the duke a shrug. "Come to Cheapside tomorrow, my dear duke. I'll explain all. Abraham, take me to my family."

Hugging his sister, seeing that she was alive and well, was even better to Edwin than shoeing his feet into sturdy boots. It just wasn't natural for a man to flop about nearly barefoot for so long.

Lillian craned her neck up to him and wrapped her arms about him. "I never cried so much. I saw the library, Mama's library, gone in a blink. I thought you were dead."

He hugged his sister, nestling her slim build in his arms. Her hair smelled of soot and her light-colored gown appeared ashen. "I would've been, if not for the Duchess of Charming."

Charlotte was right about his sister being safe. Who knew how much trouble he would've brought upon their heads if he'd kept picking at the pile of debris? "I found your glove in the chaos of Fairwilde." He kissed Lillian's brow. "I thought you were lost, too. Nearly went out of my mind with grief."

His sister's tears came hard and fast before she regained her composure, sniffling. "I'm glad for the duchess, but how did such a slight woman save big, strong you?"

Charlotte's stubborn independence had saved his life and captured his heart. Even now, thoughts of her fiery eyes and the proud lift of her chin as she bartered or demanded her way made his chest warm. The dreamer part of his brain started whipping up hope that maybe she felt the same of him, confused and hot. Well, bothered, more or less.

Not ready to confess, Edwin wiped the trail

of water from Lillian's cheeks with a handkerchief, then spun her toward the stairs leading to the bedrooms in his town home. "Take me to see Stepfather."

She nodded and took his hand. His poor sister's gown was tattered. Nothing of value could be recovered of her things from Fairwilde.

Her voice was low and trembling. "Father's not well. I put him in your room. I hope you don't mind."

"No. That's quite appropriate." The man had taken him in all those years ago, after all. "More than appropriate."

Theol stood at the top, pacing the polished floorboards. His stepbrother looked wild—disheveled hair, ripped sleeve, dust covering his fine onyx tailcoat. He looked like a ghost.

"This is your fault." He stepped toward Edwin and poked a finger in his chest. "You didn't give us enough money to properly repair the house."

Edwin's patience with the foppish man was at its end. He folded his arms. "I didn't hire the workmen or send the storm."

"How is this Edwin's fault?" Lillian's voice shook and clogged with sobs. "We need to pull together, especially if Father…"

"She's quite right. Theol, go get some sleep.

In the morning, we'll figure out what to do."

Fury colored his stepbrother's squinting eyes as he pounded a fist against his palm. "What are we to do now?"

God raineth on the just and the unjust. If He wanted Fairwilde in ruins, He made it happen. So it was fair for Him to give Edwin's heart to someone who might never have him. None of that mattered now; getting his family through this tragedy did. He rubbed his aching skull. "Theol, a good rest will do you well."

Lillian pushed past them and entered the largest bedchamber. "Behave, you two."

As she closed the door, Theol shoved him from behind. "What are you going to do to right this?"

His sore back stinging, Edwin spun and grabbed the man in a bear hug. Fumes of brandy spilled from his stepbrother's pores. "Don't make me hurt you. I know you're torn up over Fairwilde, but we shouldn't come to blows."

"If you don't commit to doing what's—" His slur was interrupted by a hiccup. —"—what's best for Fairwilde, I'll make sure you pay for it another way." He broke free, his chest heaving as if he could spit fire.

"Stepbrother, my patience is thin. For Lillian and Lord Rundle, let's not squabble."

"If my father dies, I will be Lillian's guardian. I'll choose whom she'll associate with and whom she marries, shoemaker."

"What are you saying?" Edwin stormed closer to the buffoon. "It better not be—"

"Yes, I will sell her into misery if you do not comply. You better hope my father lives long."

Fury swept through Edwin. Hands he used to make dainty creations fisted. Before he could stop, he punched the wind out of Shelby's gut, knocking him back two feet. In a blink, he towered over the Baron.

Shelby spat at him. "I'll do it, you cobbler."

"Time for you to sleep off the drink." One final blow to the man's jaw laid him out cold. Shelby fell to the floor snoring.

Never would Edwin allow anyone to hurt Lillian. He'd pay his whole fortune to prevent it. He forced air into his heaving lungs. He didn't feel triumphant beating the stupid man. No, a sense of shame came over him, followed by pity. Theol's whole life was centered on being Lord Rundle's son, his eldest. That might be ending soon.

Edwin drew his stepbrother over his shoulder. "Shelby Theol, we'll survive this. Now let's put you to bed." He spun and stopped, caught in Abraham's watchful gaze.

The butler moved up the final steps with a silver tea service. "It's a shame Lord Theol is so sleepy, sir."

Embarrassed at letting his knuckles solve

the problem, Edwin shook his head. "My temper helped."

Face heating, he pivoted to a close bedchamber and dumped his stepbrother onto the bed. Pressing his stinging fingers, he backed out and closed the door.

Abraham stood at the door to the bedchamber hosting Lord Rundle. "Your housekeeper says he's been drinking since he arrived. And Lord Theol's a mean drunk."

The butler's excellent livery no longer held any spots of dust. The man must've beat it out as soon as they arrived. At least some things could be counted on, like Abraham and his sense of order.

Edwin rubbed a hand through his own crazed hair and glanced at his torn waistcoat and blackened sleeves. "How can you look like a house didn't come down on you?"

"Mr. Cinder, we do what we must." Abraham marched closer. "And you must do that, too, not just for the Theols. Do what is best for you. The Cinders are respectable people, too." With a nod, the giant man entered the bedroom.

Edwin took a deep breath. He felt like running and changing, but he needed to see his stepfather. He'd already wasted too much time fighting with Theol.

Pushing into the room, he saw him. The man's skin looked pallid. His head and arm were bandaged.

The old fellow's eyes fluttered open. "Edwin, is that you?"

"Yes, sir." He ducked into the closet and pulled on the first tailcoat he could grab, anything to cover up his dusty attire.

"Come here, Son."

Edwin toddled out, yanking and buttoning, then moved near his sister. She sat at her father's side. They both looked so fragile.

Rundle lifted his good arm and waved it toward him. "So glad you are well. I was in anguish thinking you were hurt."

Anguish? Edwin caught the man's palm.

The old fellow coughed. "I had Abraham return and stay until they found you. He sent word that you were with the Duchess of Charming."

He tugged on his blanket and adjusted his head. "She's a good girl, but full of strong opinions like her father. You two would be a good match."

Rundle, God love him, was consistent to the end, pushing Edwin a little bit more from his comfortable notions. "You like fairy tales, but we both know those things never happen in real life. Especially for me. My bloodline isn't noble enough."

Lillian shook her head. "That's not true."

His stepfather lifted up a little. "You can't

wait for the fairy tale. You have to make it. You are capable and worthy regardless of your relations."

"Agree with him, Mr. Cinder, so he won't get so heated." The butler poured a cup of tea for Lillian. His dark eyes seemed to shine in the low light as if wet.

With another cough, Rundle lowered himself. His voice sounded weak, crumbling. "You—you have to be impassioned about truth."

Edwin wiped his brow. He needed to change the subject from his embattled heart. "Sir, I don't want you troubled about Fairwilde. I'll support you in rebuilding it."

"Fairwilde was a place for my family. There can be other places, if the family is together. I had tried to set some things in motion for you, but now the *ton* might think an association with Lord Rundle is not good."

Anger beat in Edwin's chest. No one would disparage his family. "Don't think like that. Lord Rundle is the best."

His stepfather tightened his grip on Edwin's fingers. "These hands were meant for more than slippers and boots. It's time for you to think about what you want. Life is short, unpredictable. My peace comes from knowing you will stand up as I lay down."

Edwin kept a firm hold on his stepfather, as

if that would keep the man with them, but who could fight time? Not his father or mother, and not dear Rundle.

"It's time to claim what you want, what will make you happy, Son."

Son? The dear man had repeated the word, but this time Edwin let his soul feel the love and responsibility of it.

"Think of what you want." Rundle's head leaned to one side, dipping further into the pillow.

What Edwin desired and what he thought a shoe peddler deserved had always been two separate things. "Save your strength. Next year, the Rundle party will be the best. You'll see."

"I'm not missing my next party with your mother. Ours was a love match as much as it was convenient. Take care of our family. Hold them together, even Shelby. If you hear from my youngest son, the prodigal Percival, tell him I love him too."

The weight of his words pressed upon Edwin, squeezing his chest. He couldn't breathe, just like being wedged in the coal chute. "Excuse me."

He did everything in his strength not to bolt out the bedchamber, but his feet pounded fast.

On the other side of the door, he fell into a chair. This was worse than when his natural father died. John Cinder worked hard and taught

Edwin things as a boy. Lord Rundle took that boy and made him a man.

Rocking back and forth, he swallowed the sobs gathering in his throat. Without Rundle, who would guide him, badger him into seeking relaxation or a hat? "Lord, it's me. What am I to do?"

An image of Charlotte, her smile, came to his head. Pensive, he brought his fingertips together. The flesh felt very cold, but he rubbed his palms. "Help me to know what You want with these hands. Show me. I won't scoff or disbelieve, not anymore. If You see me as a son, as worthy enough for a duchess, then that is what I am."

His chest loosened. Air went in and out of his windpipe with more ease. He stood up tall and went back into the room with the earthly father who believed in him.

Quietly as he could, he sat next to Lillian, gathered her in his arms, and let her lean upon his shoulder. "I am worthy, Step…Father. I'll do what should be done."

Lord Rundle blinked at him. His mouth widened to hold a grin. He clasped Edwin's palm, shut his lids, and slipped into peace.

CHAPTER SEVEN

Morning Calls

The morning's bright sun burned Edwin's eyes, but he still had a number of tasks to accomplish. The sky was perfect, as if rejoicing at the entry of one of its saints, dear Lord Rundle. Not a cloud shadowed his steps, so different from yesterday.

He stretched his arms and willed away the strain in his back. After waiting with the coroner, he sent footmen all over London bearing notes of apology and well-wishes to the dinner guests. Forcing Abraham to sleep late, Edwin went about getting clothes and dressmakers sent to his residence. Lillian needed a proper black dress, and Theol a new suit. Lord Rundle's family would be unified in mourning for the dear earl.

Yet, there was one final message he needed

to deliver personally. From Abraham's memory of the guest list, he'd garnered the duchess's Grosvenor Square address.

In his second best charcoal coat, he stood upon her doorstep and waited to be presented.

Marble floors and pristine statues of alabaster skin greeted him as he followed behind a footman to a parlor. Holding his breath, he traced his mother's ring, a single band of gold stashed in his pocket.

Filling his stinging lungs, he opened the door. Instead of seeing the most beautiful woman in the world, he spied a frowning older one.

"Sir, it's not yet ten. A bit early for calls."

"It is, but I had to make sure the duchess was well. It was a harrowing night, Mrs...."

"It's Miss Goodmom. Lady Charming will be down shortly."

The scowl on the woman's face indicated a deep disappointment. What had Charlotte told her? His fingers felt icy. "Is something the matter? Is something wrong with the duchess?"

"You tell me. She was very disturbed last night. I know it had to have stemmed from whatever transpired between the two of you. Were you a blackguard to my dear girl? Are you here to make amends, or to take further advantage?"

"No." His heart beat hard, and the force of

his response made her take a step backward. "I'd give my life rather than harm a hair on head."

Miss Goodman drew a handkerchief from her pocket and mopped at her eyes. "Then why was she too upset to discuss it?" The lady paced to the window and tangled her hands in the dangling sheer curtains. "It doesn't matter. I suspect her reputation will be protected this afternoon."

Was that a threat? Was some unknown force seeking to call him out? He adjusted the careful knot he'd let his valet tie. "Why is that?"

"Because Lord Cheshire will be making her an offer tonight."

"A duke's offer." His heart missed at least two beats. How was he to compete for her love now?

Charlotte sauntered into the room. Her eyes so blue, like a fresh dip into the sea, focused upon him. "Mr. Cinder, to what do we owe the pleasure?"

Her mannerisms were stiff and formal, far from the warm woman that sought his kiss, but she was exquisite. A regal dove-gray walking dress hung upon her frame, sculpted to her delicate figure. The deep aquamarine papered walls made her gold hair seem even brighter. An angel stood so close, but the pout upon her countenance meant her heart was far from him.

His pulse raced, nonetheless. Duke or no duke, he had to try to win her. His soul would never be the same if he didn't make an effort.

Miss Goodmom traipsed to the sofa and plopped onto a cushion. She tucked her dress about her short boots. The woman must have no intention of offering them privacy.

It didn't matter. Edwin was ready to shout from the rooftops his love for Charlotte. He stepped near the beautiful woman, the lass that should be his bride. "I've come to see about you."

Her rosy lips pressed to a line. "I am well. You could've sent a note. That is what distant acquaintances do. No need to *pretend* things are any different."

He looked at Miss Goodmom. He hadn't planned on spilling his innermost feelings to an audience, but what choice did he have? "I am not distant, nor do I want to be. There is a pair of shoes—"

"Oh, that is right. Our bet. Since I was correct about your sister and Lord Rundle surviving, I suppose they are mine." She held out her hands.

He reached and clasped her fingers, bare skin to bare skin, just like last night. "You were only half right. My sister is well, but my step-father..." His voice lost its vibrancy, sounding dull and sad in his own ears. "His dying wish was for me to live." He bit his lip and stared at his heart's desire. "That couldn't be, without you."

The distant look in her eyes disappeared. Her cheek trembled. "Mercy, leave us."

"But, Duchess."

Charlotte rocked her head as if to point to the door. "Please go, Miss Goodmom."

The woman's heavy footfalls finally became silent as Charlotte's companion left the room. When the door thudded closed, Charlotte neared. "Edwin, I am so sorry. I know you cared for him."

Their gazes intertwined. He felt warm, then cold, then hot.

He released one of her hands and touched a golden tendril dangling by her neck. "Those shoes should be yours. I'm ready to pay with my heart. Will you pay the rest of the bill with yours? Could you possibly love me, too?"

Charlotte was lost. She tried to be aloof, smarting over his dismissal of her last night, but one look into his searing brown eyes made her unsure of her resolve. A shiver started in her spine as he kissed her palm.

He dipped to one knee. "Love me, Charlotte, as I do you."

She tugged on the collar of his silky black waistcoat. "Get up."

"I'll ask in as many ways necessary for you to say yes. Maybe without words." He pulled her close, lifted her chin, and took her mouth. His lips were warm and demanding. Last night's sweetness of discovery, the sugar of uncertainty, had disappeared, becoming something bigger, engulfing her in fire. His fingers tightened about her waist, pulling her off the floor. Her head became dizzy, but she clung to his hard chest, returning his affection with a blaze of her own.

Gasping, he set her down. "I hope this means you love me. When we are married, you can't greet acquaintances like this."

"Married? You want to marry me? But you said—"

"If you love me as I love you, I think we should risk it. You offer kisses that sear my flesh." He mumbled her name as his lips covered hers again.

She was lost, falling into a hole, grasping onto his lapels to keep from dropping through the floor. Was this feeling real and lasting?

Eventually, he released her. "I want you to marry me, but start with saying, 'Edwin, I love you.'"

"Before I do anything, I need to know why you changed your mind. You were quite decided to forget everything."

"I've lost a lot of people who were dear to

me. With Lord Rundle's death this morning, I am determined to celebrate life." His finger traced the outline of her lips. "I can't walk away from the notion of finding love. I had to tell you the truth of my feelings, but you need to decide."

Being able to choose was important, but her head spun at this shift, the openness of his spirit. Yesterday, he seemed to bury his emotions deep within his skin. Now, he wasn't afraid to say what was in his heart. Things changed in a few hours. Would it change back and leave her more brokenhearted?

"Charlotte, you're silent. I must be rushing you. Or I'm not doing this like a gentleman would." He dropped her palm and took two steps backward. "Or have I misread things?"

The door to her sitting room opened wide. The Duke of Cheshire stood with a giggling Mercy at his side.

Her father's friend bowed as he crossed the threshold. "Duchess, Mr. Cinder. Am I intruding?"

"Is he Lady Charming?" Edwin looked at her and then at the duke. "I guess I'm leaving. I will be busy the next few days preparing for Lord Rundle's burial, so draft a note, Lady Charming, to let me know how you fair."

"Well, since you are here, I can assume our interview about your intentions to the duchess is unnecessary." The duke shifted his stance, his head swiveling from Charlotte to Edwin.

"Find me if you must, but the answers are in the duchess's capable hands."

Mercy left Cheshire and caught Edwin's deep blue-black sleeve as she hurried him to the door. "But you will send my lady the slippers she wants. Her presentation is Friday."

He looked over his shoulder. His countenance held no smile. His eyes radiated pain. "The shoes are hers. They could belong to no other."

"Good. Send them over. Bye-bye." With a shooing wave, Mercy closed the door on Edwin and took a seat in the corner.

This time Charlotte didn't care if her friend listened. She couldn't be alone with another man who wanted to marry her. She leveled her shoulders. "Lord Cheshire, should I send for refreshments?"

"No, ma'am." He moved to the walnut bookcase at the rear of the room. He took his time touching a few novels and leather-bound spines.

Charlotte rolled her eyes. Cheshire always took his time getting to the meat of what he wanted others to know. Her father found this habit bothersome. Now she understood.

Forget men. Last night, she wept over not having her feelings returned by Edwin. She awoke settled in the knowledge she'd been mistaken about him and her own raging emotions.

Yet, this morning he wanted her, claimed to love her. Because he changed his mind, she was supposed to drop everything and allow him to play with her heart again?

Pulse thrashing so loudly her ears throbbed, she dropped into the soft chaise clad in a cranberry print. Edwin did sound sincere, and his arms surrounding her felt right, but she couldn't think like that. Marriage would put a man in control of her future. She'd just become free from her father's thumb. Unless she was absolutely sure about Edwin, she couldn't weaken.

"Duchess, what did I walk in upon?" Cheshire marched closer, his boots drumming, echoing on the mahogany floor. "Did Cinder compromise you last night?"

Anger stung her eyes. "Edwin Cinder saved my life." Her tone was loud and pitchy, but she'd defend his honor. "Then I saved his."

"I am glad to hear it." The duke's deep, masculine voice didn't sound convinced. No, it sounded amused.

Charlotte cringed and closed her eyes. Every muscle in her tired arms hurt, but she forced them to cross. Fingering her clean bodice, she lifted her gaze to Lord Cheshire. "To what do I owe the pleasure of this visit?"

A half-smile covered his mouth. His blue-green eyes were framed by crinkles, as if they bore the humor of a good joke or a delicious secret. Attired in a sapphire threaded waistcoat and buff breaches, the man looked quite handsome, particularly since he, too, survived a house dropping onto his sable head.

He wandered to the window and parted the curtains, letting in half-welcoming, half-evil sunshine. "Mr. Cinder seemed quite on edge. Did you send away a new suitor?"

Blinking, she willed her muscles to obey and sat upright. "He lost his stepfather this morning. He was quite close to the man. I think that would make one terse."

"I see." The joy dropped away from Cheshire's countenance, leaving stern lines. "Rundle was an excellent man, a good mentor to Cinder. He shall be missed." He tugged on his ear and powered closer. "I think I interrupted a proposal. Is that right?"

Mercy jumped up. "No concerns to be had. I'd make sure she'd hear you out first."

Charlotte motioned with her index finger for her companion to sit. "Miss Goodmom, please. Lord Cheshire, what is your business here today? It must be urgent to keep you away from your home."

He pivoted as if to look through the window. "I've been distracted. My wife's death was a tragic accident, and it has left me with a great many things to puzzle out—particularly how to properly care for my daughter."

A lump formed in Charlotte's throat. Not another proposal? Her limbs felt even more tired. Though it would be a good match of families, marrying Cheshire would be like wedding an uncle or a brother.

With slow steps, he marched the last three feet toward her.

Don't kneel; don't do it. Don't force me to reject you, too.

From his pocket, he pulled a folded piece of parchment. "Here. This is a wedding contract that Lord Charming wanted me to review. You should have it now."

"Cheshire, you've been a dear friend to my father, but I can't accept you."

He pushed the paper into her hand. "I'm not in the bargain. I've wed once where feelings were not as they should be. Child, you are like my own daugh...sister."

"Sister?" One of her eyebrows lifted of its own volition.

"I haven't yet reached thirty-five, far too young to be put on the shelf for dusting. Just read the contract. It was drafted between your father and Lord Rundle."

Without opening it, she crushed the paper in her palm. "My father was bombastic and opinionated. He ruled every facet of my life when he was alive; do you think I will let him do it from the grave? How could I wed one of Rundle's sons? Lord Theol is impossible. The younger can't be much better."

Mercy slipped from her chair and swiveled to the door. "This seems to be a private conversation. I should—"

"Sit, Miss Goodmom!" Charlotte didn't want her tone to sound so harsh, but it was the only way to be heard over the blood rushing in her ears.

The duke neared and took the paper from her, smoothing it of wrinkles. "Your father loved you very much. He knew your title would be the object of fortune hunters, so he chose an honorable man who'd cherish your strong opinions."

He waved the paper. "Read it." His tone was firm, but kind.

He would make a good elder brother. She scanned the document, and her heart skipped a beat. The name on the contract wasn't for Shelby Theol, the Baron Rundle, or Percival Theol. It was for an Edwin Cinder. "I don't understand."

Cheshire tugged at his waistcoat. "He is the man your father thought well enough of to give his most treasured possession, his only daughter."

Every bit of air pressed out of Charlotte's

lungs. She gulped and tried to fan her face, but her arm felt numb.

Mercy traipsed to her side and took the document, her lips forming each word as she read. The woman finished, then dropped the paper. "The fellow is rich, but he's not a gentleman. The duke would sanction this?"

"The wealth eliminates fortune-hunting. A title didn't matter to Lord Charming, since he ensured the duchess had one. Mr. Cinder came to his attention with his donation of shoes from the Ella stores."

Head spinning, she gripped the arm of the chaise. "Edwin's the one who donates footwear for Papa's orphans?"

"Yes, Mr. Cinder has done so every year for the past three without any recognition. Imagine a young man who's never set foot out of London, giving to a cause inspired by your father's dream. Cinder's is a heart most worthy."

Charlotte strained to hold in her tears and rubbed her brow. "Papa chose Mr. Cinder? Does the man know his stepfather was trying to run his life?"

"I don't know, but Cinder is the right man. I think you know that, too. Someone who wouldn't use the isolation and desperation of last night to compromise you; one thinking of your reputation enough to propose—that's a good fellow."

He folded his arms as a crease formed between his eyes. "Was there something more to his proposal?"

Of course there was. It was the kiss that lingered upon her lips, the need to hear his voice low in her ears, and how in his arms she felt she belonged. She swallowed the lump in her dry throat. Her voice dropped to a whisper. "He says he loves me."

"You are smart enough to know whether or not it's true, but you are stubborn like your father. Don't reject happiness because it was condoned by Lord Charming. We fathers are sometimes right. I've done my part and informed you. You have my blessing in the choice of Cinder, if you so want it."

He plodded to the door. "Godspeed, Duchess." The duke chuckled as he slipped from the room.

When the sound of the front door shutting filled the air, Charlotte slumped her shoulders. How could Father know she'd even like Edwin? Did he coerce God into sending a storm from heaven to ensure it?

"Are you in love with Mr. Cinder?" Her friend stooped in front of her. "If you love him, then go after him. Seek his love."

"I thought you only wanted a duke."

"I know Lord Cheshire. I know how he'd treat you. I know nothing about Edwin Cinder, but if your father picked him, then he is a good man, a worthy man. You understand this, don't you?"

Charlotte choked back a sob. "Father can't be right in this."

"So you would rather be alone like me with no hopes or prospects of being a wife and mother." Mercy patted Charlotte's arm, then stood tall.

"Don't toss away a chance to be loved because the late duke agreed. Your father was a smart, caring man, and no one would ever call him stupid or a poor judge of character." She left the parlor, closing the doors behind her.

Charlotte was alone, aching on the inside and outside.

Papa chose Edwin. How could she ever be with Edwin now? That would let Papa win. She sat back on her father's chaise, in his Grosvenor Square town home, and cried until her eyes throbbed.

CHAPTER EIGHT

The Slipper

tanding in front of her mirror, Charlotte adjusted the top hoop supporting the wide skirt of her court dress. In a few more hours, she would be showing herself to the Queen of the United Kingdom, an elegant lady also gloriously named Charlotte. Swishing from side to side, she admired the ivory satin top skirt edged with garlands of pearls and stripes of crimson and gold. Decadent, almost heady. She smoothed the shiny underskirt and watched the endless white silk billow with her slight movements.

She'd do very well today attending this formal presentation, if not for the dark circles under her eyes. Two nights of not sleeping, and crying most of Wednesday and Thursday, did nothing for her complexion. Would Edwin think her pretty now or pretty foolish?

With a shake of her head, she cast aside all her doubts of letting him go and focused on keeping her shoulders level as she stepped in reverse. No one could put her back to the queen, especially a new duchess.

After her sixth try, a new sense of confidence filled Charlotte's middle, and she allowed a smile. Surrounded in such a big skirt, if she spun she'd resemble the glass top Papa bought her when they went to Venice. *Oh, Papa.* Was the toy still in her room at their country manor?

An easier breath left her. Those days with Papa and her were so simple. When she wasn't fuming over Edwin, she thought about the late duke. Yes, he was authoritative, but he had a gentle laugh and enjoyed spinning that top, playing with her.

Imagining the wobbly path of the toy, she twirled. The skirt's strings of pearls caught the air and warbled like the beats of bird wings. Lavender, her calming perfume, whipped to her nostrils as she panted and sank against her bedpost. The tinkle of bead-hitting-bead matched the thudding of her heart. She'd make Papa proud today.

Her long gloves sat on the bed next to a parcel wrapped in ice blue paper, the distinctive packaging of the Ella's shoe stores. She blew out a frustrated breath, fluttering the heavy ostrich plume decorating her chignon. The nerve of Edwin Cinder to wait until the last possible minute to send the slippers.

She shouldn't wear them. Maybe she should send them back. If it weren't for those beautiful things she wouldn't have met Edwin, wouldn't know how generous his spirit was or how self-sacrificing the man was. Indeed, she wouldn't be thinking of him night and day.

How was he? Did the impact of Lord Rundle's death sting his chest when he saw the coffin? Did his knees almost give way when he visited the freshly dug grave?

When she saw her father's grave, that's when the loss of him squeezed her heart and made her face a track for tears. She closed her eyes. It wasn't the heavy-handedness that burnt her throat; it was the loss of him. After her mother died, Papa was everything. Then he had to die and leave her, too.

He'd never see her presented at court. Never torture himself getting her ready for a season. Never offer her hand to another for a first dance. He'd never know her husband or his own grandchildren.

A knock on her door sounded. Then Mercy bounded inside. "Are you ready to leave?"

Charlotte batted her sticky lashes and mopped her face. The queen wouldn't want to be introduced to a weepy duchess.

Mercy stormed closer and adjusted pins in Charlotte's light locks. "Do you want to talk about it? It's been three days since I cast out your suitor. I shouldn't have interfered. You're miserable. "

"I was wondering if I should wear his shoes. I think I should send them back. I've a comfortable pair in my closet."

A frown enveloped her companion's face. "These came with such a price, Charlotte—a building, falling signs. You have to wear them."

They did cost too much. Two hearts, as Edwin said. She shook her head.

"You may have patience for this non-sense"—Mercy seized the package—"but I do not." Her mitts ripped it open, tossing shreds of paper everywhere. "Oh my."

"What, Mercy? What is it?"

A toothy grin swept her friend's countenance. "It's not the slippers. Well, maybe they are, but they're different."

Charlotte crept closer. The crinkled ribbons appeared the same as the ones she remembered from the glass case, but that pair had lace and crystals. These possessed a reduced number of the light gems, with pearls added in their stead. Now the slippers matched her dress perfectly.

She fingered the delicate fabric, the sturdy soles, and drummed the dangling jewels. Edwin did this for her. With all he had to do for his family during their time of loss, he still found time for her.

Dropping to her mattress, she tried valiantly to hold in her tears. She closed her eyes as Mercy stuck the slippers onto her cold feet. The quiet voice in her heart, the one she'd been more open to hearing the last couple of days, whispered, *"It's fine to love him, to be loved by him."*

Mercy smoothed her cinnamon-colored carriage dress. "Are you ready to go, Duchess?"

Charlotte popped up, grabbed a shawl, and nodded. If she opened her mouth, surely the sobs gathering inside would leak out.

Wiggling and wedging herself through the entrance of her carriage, Charlotte navigated her wide dress onto her seat. She felt numb as she tugged her lacy wrap about her, as she had done with her rescue blanket that night.

Mercy's large reticule jingled as she settled across from her. "After we are done with court today, let's say we return to Grosvenor and send a note for Mr. Cinder to call upon us."

Edwin. Her heart whimpered at the thought of him. "He might not be done with all his visitors. His stepfather's burial is today."

Mercy plucked at the curls falling from her straw bonnet. She stuck her hand deep into her bag and popped out more pins. One by one, she poked and fastened her deep brunette tresses.

The dear woman had spent so much time getting Charlotte ready she hadn't seen to her own needs. So self-sacrificing, just like Edwin.

"He may be in great need of a distraction. What do you say, Duchess?"

Unsure of what to do, Charlotte remained quiet, slouching upon the seat. Edwin delivered upon every one of his promises the night Fairwilde fell, keeping her protected underneath the rubble and getting her to safety in the cellar. Now, he offered these precious slippers, just as he said. What had she done for him?

Shame welled inside. She'd pouted instead of sending a letter, and didn't stand beside him through the loss of his stepfather as she'd promised.

Lulling notes like the strain of a waltz, similar to the harp music at the Rundle ball during her only dance with Edwin, filled the carriage. "Mercy, stop."

"Sorry, Duchess."

The humming didn't calm Charlotte's nerves or the tumult in her mind. Panting, she turned to the window. A gasp left her lips. The carriage passed in front of Fairwilde's ruins.

Before she could stop herself, she struck the ceiling.

Mercy grabbed her hand. "Charlotte, what are you doing? We'll be late."

Nothing else mattered; only a need to pace

Fairwilde's sidewalk pressed upon her lungs. Charlotte waited for the horse team to slow, then forced her skirt through the narrow door. "I need to see it."

She turned from her friend and scanned the lot where the great home once stood. Men rummaged through the debris, stacking bricks and lumber into piles. A few carts stood packed to the top with broken bits of china and marble.

Huffing, Mercy plodded next to her. "You need to head back. You could get dirty, and there won't be time to change. You won't be presented to the queen. It would be nearly impossible to get on the list again, unless you marry a nobleman." Her companion's voice vibrated through Charlotte's spine, but she wouldn't pivot.

A royal presentation, the thing she'd wanted to prove her worth, didn't matter anymore. She traipsed a little farther and noticed a man's shoe in the back of a cart of cast-offs. Edwin's?

Picking up her skirts, she wobbled and pranced in her new slippers until she approached the dray. Fingers stretching over the low fenced wall, she touched the refuse and smelled raw earth.

With another inch of reach, she'd get his slipper, the one he lost beneath the rubble. Edwin was worth the trouble, but could he forgive her? Did he still want her?

Leaning against the muddy rail stained her bodice. When she latched her pinkie onto the silver buckle and hauled the dusty shoe to her bosom, she felt at peace and in control, as she had when she'd wielded the ax to save Edwin. All Charlotte had to do was find the man who owned this slipper and convince him they still had a chance at happiness.

Edwin climbed into his carriage, following his stepbrother. They'd made it through the graveside service without squabbling. Well, maybe having a new onyx suit of the finest wool softened Shelby as much as Edwin's right cross to the man's cheek.

"Shoemaker." He sat up, arms folded over his chest. "Your workmen are clearing the land. Will you rebuild the great house, too? "

Well, so much for the truce. Edwin lifted his favorite smooth, tanned leather shoe and tossed out a pebble. As he slipped the unadorned slipper back upon his foot, he stared at his stepbrother. "No."

His stepbrother's green gaze turned to fire. His hands fisted within his gloves. "But you know how much it meant to my father and your mother."

That was a bit of gall. Shelby never cared for his stepmother and now used her memory for an advantage. Edwin heaved out a deep breath. "My mother is dead, and now Lord Rundle is, too. It's time for new dreams."

Shelby grabbed at Edwin's sleeve. "Fairwilde is all I have left of him. Don't kick me into the grave, too."

This was desperation, a familiar feeling Edwin had been fighting since Charlotte's dismissal of his love. Sighing, he reached out and batted Shelby's fingers. "You have his title. You are Lord Rundle now, the new Earl of Rundle. You must go after your own way."

Shelby grunted, lifting his long nose. "That's a useless sentiment. I haven't access to the funds I need."

"I'll help. You will stay at my home until you decide your course. I'll even give you pocket money if you stay sober. Abraham will account for it."

Shelby rubbed his brow, his shoulders slumping. "Live in Cheapside with the butler as my banker. Now I feel ill."

"Theol—Lord Rundle, there are a number of wealthy daughters of the merchant class living nearby. This might be the perfect place for you."

Shelby rolled his eyes, ducked against the seat corner, and tapped down his hat.

"You'll have the place by yourself for a while. I'm taking Lillian. We're going to travel."

"Father's not yet cold in the ground," Shelby's snide tone vibrated through his felt brim, "and you're running away."

Not taking the old bait, Edwin sat back. "I run from nothing, but I've—we've—never ventured from London. I'm going to see the world. I must make sure Lillian knows how to dream before she's grown. We'll be back in enough time for you to use your influence for her prospects when she comes of age in a year or two."

The carriage came to a stop in front of Edwin's town home. Shelby shrugged and scratched his jaw. "It's not like I could force you to stay, but if you make good on your part of keeping me in comfort, I'll see what I can do."

His stepbrother plodded outside, straight up the cobblestone path to the door. The man never looked back, but at least he didn't threaten more of his rank nonsense. Perhaps sobriety helped him realize their sister wasn't leverage. Maybe time away and Abraham's watchful eye would mellow him even more.

Edwin filled his lungs, savoring the joy of leaving London. Even in the midst of mourning and his greatest disappointment, he still had joy. That would keep him going in spite of having to endure another hour of sad faces. Hopefully, the early visitors had kept Lillian's mind occupied as the menfolk went to the burial. Footsteps pounding, he crossed the threshold and offered his hat, greatcoat, and gloves to Abraham.

The tall man took the bundle and hefted it in his large arms. The pristine cut of his dark livery and organized manners made Edwin's modest home seem special, almost like the grandeur of the lost Fairwilde.

"Mr. Cinder, many have come to offer condolences. The late Lord Rundle touched many."

Edwin filled his lungs, tweaked his snowy cravat, and brushed wrinkles from his dove-gray waistcoat. The noise of guests filtered all around from the sunny yellow parlor and tiny drawing room. Taking a few more steps, he even spied people in the corners, like the Duke of Cheshire and Charlotte....

Edwin's world stopped. The peace he'd been keeping slipped from his clutches. Had she come to announce her engagement to the duke and shred his heart anew?

Against his will, his gaze locked with hers. His mouth dried as she took a step toward him. The bright court dress of crimson and gold was out of place in the dark garbs of the mourning crowd, but her endless blue eyes, the sunshine gold of her hair, would always command attention no matter what she wore.

And on her feet were the slippers he'd remade. They fit her perfectly and matched the extravagance of her gown, pearls and all. She looked so beautiful it hurt.

Maybe he and Lillian could be out of London before any announcement of her and Cheshire's engagement made the papers. He pivoted and sought his sister. *All would work for their good*, he chanted to himself. Yes, all—even if that meant Charlotte and he wouldn't be together. God knew best and would give his child, one of his son's best. Yet, how could that not be the duchess?

Chest constricting, he shuffled his feet and moved to the window where Lillian stood. "How are you doing?"

Shrouded in black with a matching shawl, she turned from the glass. Her damp eyes blinked, then peered up at him. "People started arriving about an hour ago. Your friend, the duchess, was most kind."

Charlotte comforted Lillian?

His sister swiped at her eye. "It was nice to hear." Her sad voice, almost a whisper, shook, garbled with tears. "They don't blame Papa for what happened."

"Not for one second do you think about blame." He put his arm about her shoulders. "Who can stop a determined gale?"

"Yes, Lady Lillian, who can?" The light voice sliced another chunk from his heart. Charlotte stood at his side, the lower hoop of her bell-shaped dress brushing against his breeches. "I'd like to speak with you, if I may?"

Breathing the soft lavender scent of her hair, he rotated and dipped his head in a quick bow. "No need, ma'am. There's nothing to say. I wish you well."

Charlotte put a hand to his wrist, and a spark surged though him. "It is very important, Mr. Cinder."

The pout of her lips as she called his name was a new kind of torture. He didn't like this out-of-control feeling, or the hot frustration of seeing his heart's desire in front of him and not being able to hold her or call her his own.

Lillian patted his arm. "Go speak with her, Brother." The girl even offered him a little smile, the first in days.

Another chunk of his heart disappeared.

Words failing, he pivoted and pointed to the hall. With Charlotte's steps tapping behind him, the gentle bleating of her beaded gown, he guided the duchess into his small study.

Her long neck rose as she surveyed the modest room and trailed her smudged glove along his ordered desk. What soiled her glove and her opulent dress? Did her carriage have trouble? It wouldn't surprise him at all if she had personally overseen the repairs. Charlotte was fearless and beautiful. Oh, for her to be his. His brain must already be on holiday, for it started dreaming of a future with this special woman.

His fingers slipped down the length of the whitewashed frame, but he left the door open and stood far away from her in front of his pine bookcases. It was better to have the room accessible so passersby wouldn't think ill of her, a promised women seeking counseling from a hopelessly in love single man.

Truthfully, the lack of privacy was better for Edwin. It kept him from hauling her into the air and kissing this foolishness for the Duke of Cheshire out of her head.

The man Charlotte loved barely looked at her, but she could feel the tension in him, noticed the balling of his fingers. Was Edwin angry at her coming?

Trying to think of the right things to say, she swatted at her bodice. Even with the brown stain, her dress was too lively for mourning. She knew that, but there wasn't time to change. When she finally decided what mattered, she couldn't dawdle. "I had to see you."

He folded his arms. His deep gray waistcoat atop his dark breeches made his chest seem larger, giving her more reasons to fall into his embrace. "'Twas no need, ma'am."

"The shoes are exquisite. And the pearls, such a special touch. I must thank—"

"A promise made is a promise kept." He ran

a hand through his walnut hair before lowering it into his formal stance, arms pulled behind his back. "If you are worried I will confess to the duke about kissing you, you have my silence. I'll try to forget everything."

Forget? Her heart pounded at the notion. She swept near and put a hand on the crisp lapel of his jet tailcoat. "I can't forget. I don't want to."

"I am..." His voice grew tight and low. "I am not the kind of man to play false. Nor will I ever think of possessing anything that's not mine. Go back to your betrothed. The duke's a good *gentleman*. You'll do well by him."

Her pulse raced at his foolish notion, but it confirmed Edwin wasn't immune to this crazed feeling pumping through her veins. "I'm not engaged. Do you think I would be here, asking to see you, if I was?"

In a rush, his hands appeared at her sides, and he hovered about her as if to pull her to him, but he stopped inches from her capped sleeves. He lowered his palms. "Then you've come, to mourn with us?"

The speech she'd rehearsed in her head disappeared at the warm look in his soulful brown eyes. She stuck her palm into Mercy's reticule and brought out his shoe. "I was on my way to my presentation when Miss Goodmom and I passed Fairwilde. The workmen were busy carting off debris that used to comprise a home. I saw this shoe and thought about making my home, my place in the world. How could it not be with the man who lost this slipper saving me?"

He took it, grasping the small heel. "You didn't make your presentation? It's what you wanted. I don't understand."

"We came here instead. I knew when I saw this slipper, I had to marry the man who owned it. We didn't make it to court. I'm glad, for your sister said you both are leaving."

His fingers clasped tightly about the sole, making the slipper pucker. Its shiny buckle poked forward as if to pop free. "Yes, I wish to travel the Continent. Lillian needs to be away from all this. I do, too."

Had Charlotte hurt him too much for him to risk his heart again? She moved closer. "You've never traveled. How do you know where to go? You'll need someone to guide you."

His eyes narrowed. "We'll manage. What is it you want?"

"Marry me. You're the man who owns this shoe, the man who must belong in my life."

His eyes looked troubled, a swirling pool of delicious chocolate trouble.

"Sir, you can't tell me no, and we shouldn't wait another moment. I know now we are meant to be in love, in fellowship—married.

He laced her fingers through the crook of his arm and led her from the room. "We'll see. Come."

He mustn't believe her, but yet she followed. She lifted her chin, confident that listening to her heart would allow things to end well.

As they re-entered the parlor, Edwin's face became blank, no longer set with a frown but also without a smile. *Lord, please don't let him do something too drastic.*

Guests, mingling on his sofa alongside his dear sister or leaning the sideboard didn't move or pay attention to the stone-faced, handsome man leading her through the room, or to her wide flapping skirts.

Edwin's head whipped from side to side, even toward the entry.

Would he toss her out of his home? Her knees knocked a little, and she closed her eyes for a moment. Letting God or even Edwin lead her wasn't weakness, but a source of strength. She batted her lashes at the man she loved. "Where to?"

"There." His tone was calm, even as he whirled her toward a corner where the Duke of Cheshire and the late Lord Rundle's eldest stood. His fingers smoothed her glove and coaxed her forward. The grip balanced both a possessive strength and the acknowledgment of her own power.

She could pull away from his fingertips and stop in her path, but she didn't want to. He needed to do something, and it resonated inside her heart to trust him.

"Duke, Lord Rundle." His voice sounded pleasant, so different from in his study. "The duchess discovered a lone shoe in the rubble. I believe it's yours, stepbrother."

Blood rushed to her ears. Had she'd promised to wed Shelby Theol, the new Lord Rundle, the owner of the shoe? Never Shelby Theol! She clawed at Edwin's arm. He had to know this wasn't what she meant.

Pointing his long nose up in the air, Rundle folded his arms. "Rubbish. Kind woman, thanks. You really shouldn't have."

Edwin nodded, but his gaze seemed focused on the smaller man. "Might I buy it from you?"

Cheshire grinned. "He seems determined, Rundle. Better make a deal."

With a yawn, the new earl looked at her, then back to his stepbrother. "It's rubbish, but I'd let you have it for double my pin money."

"Done. Thank you." Edwin bowed and spun her. "Now that this is complete, let's finish our conversation, Duchess."

She gripped his arm and padded at his side.

He let her slip into his study first. The narrow passage surely wouldn't host both at the same time, not with the hoops. This time he closed the door.

Balancing on the edge of the desk, he scooped up the slipper, yanked off his low boot, and crammed his stocking foot inside. "You were saying the man who owns this shoe, or the one who fits this shoe—which would you wed?"

He hobbled closer. The slipper clearly was too small. Shifting his stance, he tottered. "Is that what the Duchess of Charming said?"

She pursed her lips, suppressing the smile attempting to form upon her countenance. "I said *owned*."

With a sigh, he kicked off the slipper. "Good. That is what I thought." Fighting through her hoops, he gripped her waist in a tight embrace, lifting her against his chest. "Just tell me you love me. Make it plain and simple for this shoe peddler."

She wrapped her arms about his neck, deflating his thin cravat, and wedged as close to him as her dress hoops would allow. "I love you, Edwin Cinder, with all my heart."

"I love you, too." His mouth took hers.

She had no complaints at the way he held her as if she'd disappear, or at the savage devouring of her kiss. She was where she wanted to be, in the arms of the man who understood her and let her choose their happy ending.

Edwin set her down and took a step backward. "We marry tonight. Let's head to Scotland. That will be the first part of our journey."

"Then off to Ireland. You can see the children you supply with shoes. Mercy Goodmom is at Grosvenor packing as we speak. She'll be a proper companion for Lillian while we seek privacy." She flashed him a purring smile, like a content kitten. "Once the mourners have left, we can be on our way."

His brow lifted. "You assumed I'd be taking you?"

She almost giggled as she smoothed her bodice. "You're not a very good negotiator, Edwin. You gave me these slippers without any concessions, and you just bartered for a single shoe for who knows how many pounds. You need me to guide you. An honest fellow can be cheated."

"I'm amazed I built such a fortune before meeting you." He folded his arms. His chestnut gaze simmered. Joy teased his large, dark irises. "How did I ever get along without you? But what if I had been stubborn, like you?"

She truly had been fighting her heart, the Lord, even her father before admitting to needing Edwin. She blinked up at him, soaking up the heat in his stare. "I was ready to pursue you. Sooner or later, you'd come to your senses and marry me."

"Oh, I see." He reached into an inner pocket of his tailcoat, pulled out a simple gold band, and slid it across her slim knuckle. "Or maybe I've just enough patience to trust that my duchess will listen inside to what's right. All will work for our good, for I love and trust God and my lady."

Had he been carrying a wedding band with him the entire time? He'd assumed she'd give in! Before she could lob a complaint, he swept her into his arms and into another enveloping kiss.

In his arms, she felt right. Her soul shouted that this was the right path. Thank God for giving her a home in Edwin's love. Hopefully, the guests would hurry and leave so they could elope and begin the rest of their lives.

Author's Notes

I enjoyed writing *Swept Away* because I believe dreams can come true and love is waiting for everyone. Stay in touch. Sign up at www.vanessariley.com for my newsletter. Let me know if you'd like to see other Regency tales.

Thank so much for giving this book a read.

Vanessa Riley

Here are my notes:

Inheritance

The rules of inheritance for titles of nobility typically dictate that the title be passed along the male lines. Upon the death of the title holder, the title passes in this order:
- Eldest son
- Eldest son's eldest son
- Eldest son's eldest son's eldest son (until there are none left)
- Second son
- Second son's eldest son (until this is exhausted)
- Any remaining son in order of birth
- Eldest brother of the title holder

- Eldest brother's eldest son (or any other son until this is exhausted)
- Second eldest brother (and so on until this is exhausted)
- Eldest surviving male descended from the original title holder

Notice the lack of females. Titles were typically passed to males, not females. However, I modeled the Duchess of Charming after the 2nd Duchess of Marlborough, Henrietta Churchill. The 1st Duke of Marlborough was given special permission in 1706 to pass his title to his daughter. He was a war hero with no living sons. She became the Duchess of Marlborough in 1722.

Storms

When reading Regencies, I love getting into the environment, learning about the land, flowers, etc. I even love being immersed in the weather.

Weather, Vanessa? Really?

Now, some might look at weather as just a scenery element, purring at the way the moonlight beams from the hero's eyes or the soft bounce of sun reflecting in the heroine's hair. However, weather can also be a force to reckon with, a third character changing the course of events.

Haven't you read about the snows of the yuletide keeping the family in the country as opposed to rushing back to London? Or the occasional rainstorm trapping the hero and heroine? You may have even read about 1816, the year with no summer.

Yet, England like most places, experienced much more. After much research, I came across two events, which occurred March 4, 1818 and April 26, 1818. The gale of March 4 raged all over England, but it also knocked over several buildings in London. The tornado of April 26 focused on the southern coast.

The March 4th Gale raged on the 4th, 7th and the 8th. The gale was likely an offshoot of a coastal hurricane, but its reach was massive. Moreover, the respite in between the 4th and the 7th fooled people into thinking the worst was over.

Here are some quotes on the event:

From the Hampshire Isle of Man and Wight Weather Book discussing the gale:

"Storm across southern Britain caused considerable damage around Nottingham, uprooting trees, blowing slates off roofs etc. At Leicester and Mansfield ... the storm was very violent, and attended with similar effects to those experienced in this town."

The Manks Advertiser and Jefferson's Intelligencer, A Douglas, England Newspaper from March 5th, 1818 says:

"We have not for many years witnessed so tremendous a storm as last night struck terror into every bosom and, carried havoc and devastation in its train."

"It had been thundering; and lightning and blowing strong for several days previously, and consequently the harbour at Douglas was crowded with shipping of all sizes. On Wednesday, the 4th, the wind stood at sou'-west, but at night it suddenly veered to sou'-east, and then blew a hurricane. Scarcely a vessel in the port escaped."

"Neither cable nor post resisted the storm the very posts in the quay were dragged cut."

"A brig, Samuel, of Whitehaven, entered the harbour, and, driven by the gale, crashed into the other vessels. Then ensued crashing and smashing and fearful confusion — masts and bowsprits snapped, bows and sterns stove in, bulwarks smashed. Two boats were actually sunk; no lives lost, but many persons were injured. The quays were crowded with people, and everyone who had a lantern brought it to the quayside."

References:

Davison, M., Currie, I. and Ogley, B. 1993. *The Hampshire and Isle of Wight Weather Book*. Froglets Publications and Frosted Earth, Froglets Publications Ltd., Brasted Chart, Westerham, Kent, TN16 1LY. Paperback, 168pp. By Mark Davison, Ian Currie and Bob Ogley.

(1818, March 5) Storm. The Manks Advertiser And Jefferson's Weekly Intelligencer. P3.

http://www.phenomena.org.uk/page29/page46/page46.html

http://www.southampton.ac.uk/~imw/jpg-Ches

il/5CH-1824-Hurricane-map.jpg
    http://www.isle-of-man.com/manxnotebook/ful
ltext/mxa1901/ch09.htm

Glossary

The Regency – The Regency is a period of history from 1811-1825 (sometimes expanded to 1795-1837) in England. It takes its name from the Prince Regent who ruled in his father's stead when the king suffered mental illness. The Regency is known for manners, architecture, and elegance. Jane Austen wrote her famous novel, *Pride and Prejudice* (1813), about characters living during the Regency.

England is a country in Europe. London is the capital city of England.

Abigail – A lady's maid.

Soiree - An evening party.

Bacon-brained – A term meaning foolish or stupid.

Bombazine – Fabric of twilled or corded cloth made of silk and wool or cotton and wool. Usually the material was dyed black and used to create mourning clothes.

Breeches - Short, close-fitting pants for men, which fastened just below the knees and were worn with stockings.

Compromise - To compromise a reputation is to

ruin or cast aspersions on someone's character by catching them with the wrong people, being alone with someone who wasn't a relative at night, or being caught doing something wrong. During the Regency, gentlemen were often forced to marry women they compromised.

Dray - Wagon.

Footpads – Thieves or muggers in the streets of London.

Greatcoat – A big outdoor overcoat for men.

Pelisse - An outdoor coat for women that is worn over a dress.

Quizzing Glass – An optical device similar to a monocle, which is typically worn on a chain. The wearer might use the quizzing glass to look down upon people.

Reticule – A cloth purse made like a bag that had a drawstring closure.

Season – One of the largest social periods for high society in London. During this time, a lady attended a variety of balls and soirees to meet potential mates.

Ton – Pronounced *tone*, the *ton* was a high class in society during the Regency era.

Excerpt *Madeline's Protector*
Chapter 1

Shropshire, England, Iron Country, August 5, 1821

"Stop, thief!" Madeline St. James grabbed the coarse sleeve of the man who stole her guineas, but he shook free and dashed away.

"Give those back, this instant." Mouth open, pulse racing, she stopped her pursuit. A scream bubbled in the pit of her stomach, but she pursed her lips. A St. James never made a public scene or conceded defeat.

The thief reached the other side of the vacant courtyard, well ahead of a wagon rumbling up the cobblestone lane. He shot her a toothless grin and traipsed to the main building of Tilford Coaching Inn.

The dray and its lumbering horse team swerved closer, but if she waited one more second, the thief would escape her view. Another man would've taken advantage of her. Not again.

Picking up her weighty skirts, she sprinted onto the slick rocks of the road. The silver hem of her long carriage dress slapped at the mud. Better to be dirty than a victim. Cupping her palm to her eyes, she scanned for the thief.

The man bounded up the stone entree. He'd vanish like her driver, amongst the sea of gaming travellers.

She lengthened her stride to intercept him.

One high step too many, her boot heel caught in the sagging silk, tripping her. The air pushed from her lungs as she fell flat. The soggy earth saturated her layers to the shift and petticoat. Her injured elbow stung anew.

Wheels squealed. Hooves clomped the cobbles. Soon the horses would be on top of her, stomping and kicking.

A couple of tugs and yanks couldn't fish her boot free. No escape this time. *Abba Father, forgive.* She turned her head and braced for the onslaught.

A band of iron gripped her stomach and hauled her from the muck. She went limp, sprawled against the hard chest of a rescuer. He pulled her off the lane and under one of the overhanging galleries of the inn.

Wind slapped her cheek as the horses swept past. No one held the reins. The wagon swung wide, crashed into the inn's main building, and flipped to the ground. Ejected barrels hit the whitewashed wall and sprayed foamy liquid.

Madeline's breath came in heaves, and she clutched the titan arm sheltering her. *No fainting. No need to lose more dignity.*

One of the draught horses loosed from its tether and galloped to the emerald pines scalloping the surrounding hills. The other roan remained with the wreck, lifting its crooked leg. Poor lame creature.

An old man rushed out of the inn and cut at the horse's strap. "Bring my gun. This one needs to be put down."

With an awkward hold on her middle, her rescuer spun her, perhaps to keep her from seeing the cruelty. He needn't be concerned.

The past two weeks had numbed her to violence. Yet, God kept her as He did again today. "Thank you, Providence, but please...spare the roan."

"You're welcome, but it's Devonshire, Lord Devonshire." The low voice kissed her ear, heated the pulsing vein along her throat.

How could this man sound calm? They both could've died.

He flung open the door to an onyx carriage and eased her onto the floorboards. "Are you injured, miss?"

"No." She rubbed her arms and gazed at her rescuer. He was very tall, enough to make her feel dainty even at her Amazon height. With broad shoulders and a solid chin, she couldn't have sculpted a more perfect hero. "The horse, sir? Can you help it?"

"Stay put. This mere mortal will see what can be done." He grabbed his top hat from the seat and marched away. His elegant form, straight posture, disappeared into the growing crowd.

It didn't matter she sat on the floor, chilled in her clothes, imposing demands of a stranger. Even against this errant horse, Death shouldn't win. She'd seen its victories too often, with Mama's passing seven years ago and Cousin Thomas dying this past spring.

She squeezed her throbbing elbow. Falling aggravated the sprain.

A quick shake of her foot didn't release her trapped kid boot but tore the lace trim on her gown, Mama's carriage dress. A lump formed in Madeline's throat. She missed Mama so much.

A few choice words shouted from the crowd and a round of loud snickers interrupted her woolgathering.

Lord Devonshire returned and rubbed the scruff of his neck. "It cost three guineas, but your nag will be kept by the innkeeper's daughter."

"I'll repay you, sir. My abigail has my reticule." She swallowed gall. The thief took most of her money, but surely three coins were left.

He waved his hand. "I'd rather not be a paid fool." Leaning along the door, he stared at her with irises bluer than a summer day.

What could Lord Devonshire learn from her disheveled appearance? She didn't mind his gaze. Since travelling to Shropshire, grey ash painted the clouds, no doubt from the ore foundries. No sunny skies like Hampshire.

"Now to be of true assistance." He reached under her hem, gripped above her ankle, and freed her boot from the tangle of silk. The warmth arising from his gloved hands seared her thin stockings. "Not broken." He released her foot to dangle through the entrance.

Shocking and bold. Though dressed as a gentleman in buff buckskins and an azure tailcoat, this definitely wasn't someone with whom to be alone.

Her wits returned, and she bounced out of the carriage. "I'll get your payment."

"Wait." Deep and commanding like Father's voice, his words stopped her. "I saw you trip trailing the miner."

She pivoted and clasped her hands across her ruined pelisse. Mud covered the delicate puce rosettes embroidered on the bodice.

"You were very brave to run after him."

"Bacon-brained would be a more apt description." A raindrop splashed her forehead. Her bonnet must have fallen in the commotion. She wiped her brow. The cold balm of mud smoothed against her skin. Her heart sunk, and she wrenched off her soiled gloves. If her cheeks weren't already scarlet, they should be.

He shortened the distance between them, a smile tugging at his full lips. "In mining country, the strikes have set everyone on edge. Some resort to crime. There's a would-be highwayman on every corner. You must take care around Tilford."

A fortnight ago, his concern might've warmed her, but not now.

"Father of Heav'n!" Mrs. Elsie Wilkins, Madeline's abigail, ran to her.

"Y' weren't to leave the livery." The good woman wrapped her stubby arms about Madeline's hips. "Too much for m' heart."

In vain, Madeline pushed at Mrs. Wilkins's indigo redingote to keep it from soiling, but no force could stop the woman's bear-like embrace.

Madeline's trampled bonnet peeked from the motherly woman's reticule. Dredged in dirt, the hat's ostrich plume lay crooked. Even in haste, her abigail took care of Madeline.

With another clench, Mrs. Wilkins finally let go. "Y' face?" She yanked from her pocket a crimson cloth and scrubbed Madeline's chin.

Madeline clasped her friend's wrist. "Dear, hand me my scarf. I'll do it."

Mrs. Wilkins shook her head and kept swatting the mud. She didn't want to come on this adventure, but how could Madeline be without her strongest ally? It must be the Irish blood bubbling in the abigail's veins, making her so loyal.

"First a broken wheel, now this." Mrs. Wilkins added a spit shine to Madeline's cheek then pivoted to Lord Devonshire. "The stable boys said ye saved her. Bless ye."

"I...I saw the lass fall in the path of the wagon. I am the Earl of Devonshire. Very glad to be of assistance." An unreadable expression set on his countenance as he flicked a rain droplet from his sleeve. "Are there others in your party?"

"There's me—Mrs. Wilkins—and my lady, Miss Madeline St. James." She stretched on tiptoes and picked at Madeline's unraveling chignon, reseating pins and tucking tresses. "And m' lady's driver, but he disappeared, the no good lout."

Great. Mrs. Wilkins just confirmed they were alone. Now he'd be obliged to help. Indebted to a man. Could this day get any worse?

The earl rubbed his jaw. His gaze seemed locked on the colourful scarf.

Another drip from the overcast skies splattered and curled into the sable-brown hair peeking beneath Lord Devonshire's brim. He was too fine looking, too virile to be trusted. Step-mother's nephew, the handsome Mr. Kent, imparted that lesson before Madeline left home.

"Mrs. Wilkins, hand me my coins. I need to repay his lordship."

"No, miss. 'Tis my duty to escort you to your destination."

Madeline shook her head. "'Unnecessary."

"Cheshire. Please take us there." Mrs. Wilkins dabbed at her coat. "Like a divine appointm'nt, the earl being here."

"I can't speak for divinity, but you might say I've been waiting on a sign." He slipped the cloth from Mrs. Wilkins and waved it like a flag. "Someone brave to show me the way."

"I suppose we have no choice." Madeline snatched it from him with trembling fingers. She may be bacon-brained but not helpless or a plaything.

"There's always a choice. Like should I chase a scoundrel or let you freeze?"

She stilled her shaking palms.

He stepped near, removed his tailcoat, and draped it onto her shoulders. With his thick thumbs, he flipped the collar's revers to cradle her neck. His touch was gentle. "This should stop your shivers. I'll have my Mason get blankets."

Hugging herself beneath the weighty wool, Madeline gaped at Lord Devonshire. "Sir, we haven't agreed."

"The drizzle will get worse." He rotated to Mrs.

Wilkins. "The young lady was just in my Berlin. Perhaps the visit was too short to attest to its comfort."

Trimmed in gold, the carriage could overshadow her father's. Either the earl possessed great wealth or liked the appearance of it. In her experience, both conditions made men pompous or cruel. She rubbed her elbow again.

Mrs. Wilkins curtsied. "My lord, we've two trunks in the stables with our brok'n carriage."

The earl nodded, opened the door to his Berlin, and then plodded the long lane toward the livery of the coaching inn. Was it confidence or arrogance squaring his shoulders?

He didn't pivot to check on them, not once. Arrogance.

"Come along, Lady Maddie. Don't get stubborn. Remember *your* plan."

Madeline raised her chin, grasped Mrs. Wilkins's forearm, and lumbered toward Lord Devonshire's carriage. "Another obstacle to peace."

Her friend's cheeks glowed. "The beginning of peace, child. It's the beginning."

If only Mrs. Wilkins could be right. The unease in Madeline's spirit disagreed.

****

The temptation to look back almost overtook Justain Delveaux, the Earl of Devonshire. He strode faster to the livery. The girl had been spooked. If he seemed anxious, she'd run.

A fire of independence burned in her jade eyes. He'd have to placate Miss St. James and win her trust. Then she'd lead him to the killer.

At the entry of the hay-filled livery, his driver brushed Athena, Justain's filly. "Sir, are you ready to give up? The informant isn't going to show."

Justain stroked Athena's thick ebony coat, a shade lighter than Miss St. James's raven locks. "He didn't. *She* did. Look behind me. Are ladies entering my Berlin?"

Mason squinted. "Yes."

"The young one possesses the red cloth signal. She's the informant."

Furrowing his brows, Mason shrugged. "You and your jokes, sir."

"I'm serious. We're taking them to Cheshire, probably a clandestine meeting. Never thought to look for a woman. Well, not for an informant. The lass will lead me to lynch—"

"Must you wax poetic?" Mason chortled. "Genteel women shouldn't be left here, but..."

"Just say it."

"We need to leave, sir. Something's afoot." Mason wiped water from the brim of his tricorn. "The miners say a blood vengeance rides tonight."

"We'll leave soon, with my new acquaintances."

Why was Mason hedging his words? Since Justain was knee-high, the man never held his tongue.

Rain fell in buckets. Justain moved under the stable's roof.

Mason and Athena followed. He searched his blue-black flap coat and retrieved his treasured silver flask and Justain's bottle of tincture. "The filly's cut is sealed."

"Superb, but no more of this." Justain pocketed the tincture. "Put away your spirits and say your peace."

"This chase won't bring Lord Richard back." His driver's voice grated like a rebuke from the old man, Justain's father. "You've other things to contend."

Justain concentrated on the steady rhythm of the shower. It blocked the memory of Richard's last breath and Justain's mounting guilt. He was to blame for Richard dying. Nothing took precedence over avenging his brother.

"Send blankets to my guests. Have the stable grooms load Miss St. James's trunks." He trudged toward the Berlin. This couldn't be a fool's errand. He hated being a fool.

****

Madeline forced a smile at Lord Devonshire as he leapt into the Berlin. He sat in the opposing seat, tossed his sodden top hat and gloves onto the floorboards, then pushed wet hair from his face. The rain poured hard minutes after she and Mrs. Wilkins entered his carriage, and it hadn't lessened.

Seeing him soaked eased her slight agitation at him.

"Thank ye, for savin' m' mistress." Mrs. Wilkins snuggled into the corner of his carriage, her greying red curls rested upon the creamy silk lining the walls. "Ye gen'rous to escort us to Cheshire." She yawned then winked at Madeline. "So noble and so handsome."

Heat crept up Madeline's neck. She didn't need to be reminded of his looks or his bravery. "We are grateful."

"Be at ease. It's not often I play the hero these days." His sable-brown mop shadowed a lean nose and tanned cheeks. "The escapade gave me needed exercise."

At least, he remained humoured. Gratitude should weigh on her spirit, but was his deed happenstance or had he followed her? Miles and miles from Hampshire, and the feeling of being chased refused to quit.

A servant stuck his head inside the carriage. Rain drizzled down his uniform causing the braiding on his mantle to droop. "To Cheshire, my lord?"

Twisting a signet ring, Lord Devonshire glanced toward Madeline and Mrs. Wilkins and then turned to the opening. "Yes, Mason, I haven't changed my mind. My guests have gone to great lengths to find me. I shan't forsake them."

What? Why did the earl think she sought him? What tales men must feed each other.

"Yes, my lord." The frowning servant nodded and shut the heavy door.

Madeline smoothed her bodice, trying to calm the tickle in her stomach. Father told her every kindness held a price. She'd paid enough for trusting Mr. Kent. The pain from his blows to her side persisted.

"Lord Devonshire, we haven't departed. Pray help us hire a post chaise to ferry my abigail and me to my aunt?"

"No. I will see this through." He cleared his throat. "I look forward to our conversation."

Though the earl's countenance appeared pleasant with his lips curling, he fidgeted his wilted cravat. Dried, the neckcloth might've held a little height in a fashionable sense. Was he one of those pompous dandies? Her scarlet handkerchief did hold his interest.

No. If he were, the earl would've let Madeline die than risk wrinkles to his clothes. The parade of fortune hunters Step-mother marched through Avington Manor surely would've made no effort. The shrewish woman probably hoped the flock of peacocks supping at their home could convince

Madeline to accept her nephew for a mate, a lesser of evils.

The carriage lurched forward. Lord Devonshire reclined as if he posed for a portrait. His steady gaze set upon her.

Did he want his jacket returned? Did her slipping bonnet offend him? She righted it and smoothed its bent feather. "May I at least reimburse the livery expenses for my carriage?"

"Keep your precious gold coins. 'Tis my honour to serve you, Miss St. James." He grinned. Smooth white teeth peeked. "The opportunity to pull a headstrong beauty from harm's way is something I relish."

"Would you let a thief abscond with your coins?"

His smile dissolved. "No. I protect what is mine, and I'll avenge what is stolen."

Few had the patience for her opinions. She rolled one of the silver buttons of his jacket along her thumb.

"Praise be unto Prov..." Mrs. Wilkins snorted a harsh noise, her chin bobbling in the throes of sleep. With a fold and a tuck, Madeline secured the dear woman's blanket then tugged a book from the abigail's reticule.

"You two are my first guests in this new coach." The earl's tone was low.

He needn't be concerned about awakening Mrs. Wilkins. After this harrowing day, wild elephants couldn't rouse her.

Slumping near the window, Madeline glanced at the retreating landscape, the evergreens reflecting in the puddles. She'd enjoy nature now, before they crossed the Severn Gorge. Seeing the bottomless chasm would rattle her frayed nerves. The last time, ten years ago, she took this route with her parents and had curled next to Mama and hid within the folds of her shawl. *Abba Father, please allow each of my steps to be surefooted. Tell Mama I miss her.*

Lord Devonshire inched closer. Though the carriage rocked with each clip-clop of the horse team, he didn't sway. His tall frame sat erect like a sleek marble sculpture. "Is there anything I can do to make you comfortable?"

Mrs. Wilkins's bonnet fell onto her lap, her snores bleating to an embarrassing high pitch. The symphony of snoots quieted, but not before one protracted trumpet.

"No, sir." Madeline's cheeks warmed. Explaining her hasty exodus from Avington would lower his opinion of her, not that she needed his good opinion.

Egad. Step-mother was right. Madeline did over think things. She yanked her bookmark, flipped a few pages, and tried to lose herself in the passage.

He rapped the book and lowered it. "You'll ruin your sight, reading all the way to Cheshire. At our next stop, I'll have a lantern set down, unless I can capture your interest."

Another opportunist. Yes, he'd saved her from being trampled, but he was still a man. Did they do anything but seek their own pleasures? Like Mr. Kent.

Kent's sibilant whispers turned to yells ringing in her ear. He threatened to kill her for refusing his proposal. What type of life would she have if she'd eloped with a man of such vile temperament? She shuddered. Shoving her novel in Kent's eye darkened it and helped her escape.

"Miss St. James? Are you well?"

"Yes." She glanced at her wet hero. "You must be cold. I should return this." She lifted the tailcoat an inch and an ache rippled along her elbow. She clenched her teeth and let the jacket fall back to her shoulders.

"Just damp." He whipped his sleeves, rustling ivory buttons. "You seem to favour your right arm. Did I injure you in our last embrace?"

"No...no, my lord." Her breath hitched, and she sniffed an odour similar to fresh dye. It reeked. She huddled deeper in the tailcoat and swathed her nostrils. The mild fragrance of sandalwood lingered in Lord Devonshire's jacket. Peace reined in every storm, and this one smelled of safety, like her father's robes.

The earl shifted his boots hard onto the floor. "Some say confession is good for the soul. Do tell. Why were you at Tilford—a gaming den, no less?"

Madeline wobbled on the tufted cushion. "My carriage broke down. One usually has no choice where this happens."

"And your driver's missing? Such a fanciful story. I love a quality Banbury." He folded his arms like a solicitor in the midst of an inquiry. "Are you running from or to someone?"

"*To* my aunt in Cheshire, Lady Cecil Glaston. She's to tour Italy with me." Well, it would be the plan once Madeline convinced the art patroness. Madeline intended to sculpt such a stirring picture, Aunt would be anxious to see Michelangelo's *David* and abandon holding a matchmaking season. After Mr. Kent's betrayal, Madeline wasn't ready to belong to any man.

"I think you are running from someone whose wrath you fear. Don't lose courage. So much trouble is wrought from silence." For one second, the earl's sky-blue pools seemed to ripple with hurt before he blinked them clear. "We mustn't allow this."

She squinted at Lord Devonshire. Could he know she'd kept quiet about Mr. Kent?

"Help me, Miss St. James, my brave lass?"

Madeline's heart responded to the plea, thundering within her ribs, but could she be of aid without inviting Kent's revenge?

Lord Devonshire reached for her hand. "Tell me your secret. My dear, you can trust me."

Go to **VanessaRiley.com** or
ChristianRegency.com to find out more

Other Fairwilde Reflection Tales

At the Edge of a Dark Fores,
by Connie Almony–February 2014
Carly Rose contracts to live with Cole Harrison, an Iraq war vet, to train him how to use her new prototype prosthetics, only to discover the darkness that wars against the man he could become.

Red and the Wolf
by June Foster–March 2014
Newspaper reporter Lilly *Red* Hood forgot her dinner date with Handsome Hunter Woods, thanks to ADD she's had since childhood. In Hunter's absence, fellow reporter Wolf Skinner moves in with less than honorable intentions. When Lilly gets lost in the Alabama forest, which of these men will be her hero?

Mirror Mirror
by Mildred Colvin–September 2014
Can anything else go wrong? Sonya White's beloved stepmother has cancer, she is told Eric Price, the man she loves is after her family's money, then it appears someone wants her dead. She runs—right into the enemy's clutches.

Mountain of Love and Danger
by Gail Palotta–October 2014

Jack Greenthumb's having fun—a different day—a different girl. Then his dad's farm's destroyed; the girl he really loves, kidnapped. Thrust into manhood and bravery, Jack spies on criminals, scales a treacherous mountain and confronts a giant to set things right before everything's ruined.

See more at www.infinitecharacters.com.

CPSIA information can be obtained
at www.ICGtesting.com
Printed in the USA
LVHW010254250222
711932LV00007B/1205